LILY TUCK is the author of four previous novels, a collection of short stories and a biography. Her most recent novel *The News from Paraguay* won the National Book Award. She lives in New ... ty.

From the reviews of *I Married You for Happiness*:

'... es so tenderly, but without sentimentality, what it is to be ... ng and happy marriage ... Lily Tuck has written an ele- ... original work which memorializes how two ordinary lives ... ether.'   VICTORIA BEALE, *Independent on Sunday*

'... egant vigil ... a poised, readable, immediate novel.'
                                            KATE KELLAWAY, *Observer*

'One of the most beautiful love songs in novel form you'll ever read ... Tuck is a genius with moments and with beauty ... Her a'... to capture beauty will remind readers of Margaret Your- ... and Marguerite Duras.'

                        SUSAN SALTER REYNOLDS, *Los Angeles Book Review*

'... mourning, the only comfort of science is to assert the un- ... ainty of all that appears real. And perhaps that is what this ... ght, plangent novel is telling us: that character is unreadable, ... at memory is perilous.'   COLIN THUBRON, *New York Times*

Interviewing Matisse, or The Woman Who Died Standing Up
The Woman Who Walked on Water
Siam, or The Woman Who Shot a Man
Limbo, or Other Places I Have Lived
The News from Paraguay

I MARRIED YOU FOR HAPPINESS

LILY TUCK

FOURTH ESTATE • London

Fourth Estate
An imprint of HarperCollins *Publishers*
77–85 Fulham Palace Road
Hammersmith, London W6 8JB

This Fourth Estate paperback edition published 2013
1

First published in the United States by Atlantic Monthly Press

A catalogue record for this book is available from the British Library

ISBN 978-0-00-744978-1

Printed and bound in Great Britain by Clays Ltd, St Ives plc

In memory of
Edward Hallam Tuck

We never keep to the present. We recall the past; we anticipate the future as if we found it too slow in coming and were trying to hurry it up, or we recall the past as if to stay its too rapid flight. We are so unwise that we wander about in times that do not belong to us, and do not think of the only one that does; so vain that we dream of times that are not and blindly flee the only one that is. The fact is that the present usually hurts.

—Blaise Pascal, *Pensées* (#47)

There is nothing more terrorising than the possibility that nothing is hidden. There's nothing more scandalous than a happy marriage.

—Adam Phillips, *Monogamy*

I MARRIED
YOU FOR
HAPPINESS

His hand is growing cold; still she holds it. Sitting at his bedside, she does not cry. From time to time, she lays her cheek against his, taking slight comfort in the rough bristle of unshaved hair, and she speaks to him a little.

I love you, she tells him.

I always will.

Je t'aime, she says.

Rain is predicted for tonight and she hears the wind rise outside. It blows through the branches of the oak trees and she hears a shutter bang against the side of the house, then bang again. She must remember to ask him to fix it—no, she remembers. A car drives by, the radio is on loud. A heavy metal song, she cannot make out the words. Teenagers. How little they know, how little they suspect what life has in store for them—or death.

They may be drunk or stoned. She imagines the clouds racing in the night sky half hiding the stars as the car careens down the dirt road, scattering stones behind it like gunshot. A yell. A rolled-down window and a hurled beer can for her to pick up in the morning. It makes her angry but bothers him less, which also makes her angry.

A tune begins going round and round in her head. She half recognizes it but she is not musical. *Sing!* he sometimes teases her, *sing something!* He laughs and then he is the one to sing. He has a good voice.

She leans down to try to catch the words:

> *Anything can happen on a summer afternoon*
> *On a lazy dazy golden hazy summer afternoon*

She is almost tempted to laugh—*lazy, dazy?* How silly those words sound and how long has it been since she has heard them? Thirty, no, forty years. The song he sang when he was courting her and a song she has rarely heard before or since. She wonders whether it is a real one or a made-up one. She wants to ask him.

Gently, with her index finger, she turns the gold band on his ring finger round and round. Her own ring is narrower. Inside it, their names are engraved in an ornate script: *Nina* and *Philip*. Over time, however, a few of the letters have worn off—*Nin* and *Phi i*. Their names look like mathematical symbols—how fitting that is.

Nothing is engraved inside his ring. The original ring slipped off his finger and disappeared into the Atlantic Ocean while he was sailing alone off the coast of Brittany one summer afternoon.

A lazy dazy golden hazy—the tune stays in her head.

In the morning when he leaves for work, Philip kisses her goodbye and in the evening, when he returns home he kisses her hello. He kisses her on the mouth. The kiss is not passionate—although, on occasion, it is playful, and he slips his tongue in her mouth as a reminder of sorts. Mostly, it is a tender, friendly kiss.

How was your day? he asks.

She shrugs. Always something is amiss: a broken machine, a leak, a mole digging up the garden. She never has enough time to paint.

Yours? she asks.

What was his answer?

Good?

He is an optimist.

We had a faculty meeting. You should hear how those new physicists talk! Philip shakes his head, taps his forehead with his finger. Crazy, he says.

But Philip is not crazy.

Despite the old saying—said by whom?—about how mathematicians are the ones who tend to go mad while artists tend to stay sane.

Logic is the problem. Not the imagination.

* * *

With her fingers, she traces the outline of his lips. Her head fills with images of bereaved women more familiar than she is with death. Dark-skinned, Mediterranean women, women in veils, women with long messy hair, passionate, undignified women who throw themselves on top of the bloody and mutilated corpses of their husbands, their fathers, their children, and cover their faces with kisses then, forcibly, have to be torn away as they howl and curse their fate.

She is but a frail, wan ghost. With her free hand, she touches her face to make sure.

On their wedding day, it begins to rain; some people say it is good luck, others say they are getting wet.

She is superstitious. Never, if she can help it, does she walk under a ladder or open an umbrella inside the house. As a child she chanted, *Step on a line, break your father's spine.* Even now, as an adult, she looks down at the sidewalk and, if possible, avoids the cracks. Habits are hard to shed.

He is not superstitious. Or if he is, he does not admit to it. Superstition is unmanly, medieval, pagan. However, he does believe in coincidence, in good luck, in accidents. He believes in chance instead of cause and effect. The probable and not the inevitable.

What is it he always says?

You can't predict ideas.

The rain has briefly turned into snow. Flurries—most un-seasonal for that time of year. She worries about her shoes. White high-heel satin shoes with little plastic pink rosebuds clipped to the front. Months later, she tries to dye the shoes black but they come out a dirty brown color.

She should have known better. Black is achromatic.

A country wedding—small and gloomy. The tent for the reception, set up on her parents' lawn, is not adequately heated. The ground underfoot is soggy and the women's shoes sink into the grass. The guests keep their coats on and talk about the U-2 pilot who was shot down that day.

What is his name?

Mark my word, there's going to be U.S. reprisals and we're going to have a nuclear war on our hands, she overhears Philip's best man say.

Someone else says, Kennedy's hands are tied as are McNamara, George Ball, Bundy, and General Taylor's.

The best man says, Kennedy is a fool.

What else can he do? a woman named Laura asks him.

Don't forget the Bay of Pigs. Our fault entirely, the best man replies. He is getting angry.

Let's not talk politics. We are at a wedding. We are supposed to be celebrating, remember? Laura says. She, too, sounds angry.

Laura, the last she has heard, is living in San Francisco with another woman who is a potter. The best man was killed in an avalanche. He was skiing in powder down the unpatrolled backside of a mountain in Idaho with his fourteen-year-old daughter. She, too, was killed. Her name was Eva Marie—named after the actress, she supposes.

Anything can happen on a summer afternoon

Stop, she thinks, putting her hands to her ears.

Rudolf Anderson—the name of the U-2 pilot who was shot down.

Strange what she remembers.

How, for instance, once, in Boston, when she was in college, she caught sight of Fidel Castro. She still remembers the excitement of it. Dressed in his olive green fatigues, he had looked good then. He was thirty-three years old and he wore his hair long and sported a shaggy beard. Catching her eye, he smiled at her. Of this she is certain. But she was not a true radical; on the contrary, looking back, she appeared timid.

Pretty and timid.

Again she thinks about those dark-skinned, Mediterranean women, women in veils, women with long messy hair, and she wishes she could beat her breast and wail.

For their honeymoon, they go to Mexico, to look at butterflies.

Butterflies? Why? Nina tries to object.

Monarch butterflies. Millions of them. It's still early in the migratory season, but I've always wanted to see them. And afterward we can go to the beach and relax, Philip promises.

The car, an old Renault, is rented, and the roads are narrow and wind steeply around the Sierra Chincua hills as they drive from Mexico City to Angangueo. There are few cars on the road; the buses and trucks honk their horns incessantly and do not signal to pass. There are no signs for the town.

Donde? Donde Angangueo? Philip repeatedly shouts out of the car window. Standing by the side of the road, the children stare at him in mute disbelief. They hold up iguanas for sale. The iguanas are tied up with string and are said to be good to eat.

Supposedly they taste like chicken, Philip says.

How do you know? Nina asks.

Instead of replying, Philip reaches for her leg.

Keep your hands on the wheel, Nina says, pushing his hand away.

In Angangueo, they stay in a small hotel off the Plaza de la Constitución; there are no other tourists and everyone stares at them. Before they have dinner, they go and visit the church. On an impulse, Nina lights a candle.

For whom? Philip asks.

Nina shrugs. I don't know. For us.

Good idea, Philip says and squeezes her shoulder.

The next morning, when they get out of bed, their bodies are covered with red bites. Fleas.

Following the hired guide, they hike for over an hour along a winding, narrow mountain path, always going up. They walk single file, Philip ahead of her. Tall and thin, Philip walks with a slight limp—he fell out of a tree and broke his leg as a child and the tibia did not set properly—which gives him a certain vulnerability and adds to his appeal. Occasionally, Nina has accused him of exaggerating the limp to elicit sympathy. But most of the time, his limp is hardly noticeable except when he is tired or when they argue.

The day is a bit overcast and cool—also they are high up. Eight or nine thousand feet, Philip estimates. Hemmed in by the tall fir trees, there is no view. It is humid and hard to breathe. How much farther? She wants to ask but does not when all of a sudden the guide stops and points. At first, Nina cannot see what he is pointing at. A carpet of orange on the forest floor. Leaves. No. Butterflies. Thousands and thousands of them. When she looks up, she sees more butterflies hanging in large clusters like hives from tree branches. A few butterflies fly listlessly from one tree to another but mostly the butterflies are still.

They look dead, she says.

They're hibernating, Philip answers.

On the way back to town, Philip tries to explain. There are two theories about how those monarch butterflies always return to the same place each year—amazing when you think that most of them have never been here before. One theory says that there is a small amount of magnetite in their bodies, which acts as a sort of compass and leads them back to these hills full of magnetic iron, and the second theory says that the butterflies use an internal compass—

Nina has stopped listening. Look. She points to some brilliant red plants growing under the fir trees.

Limóncillos, the guide says and makes as if to drink from something in his hand.

Sí, Nina answers. By then she is thirsty.

From Angangueo, they drive to Puerto Vallarta, where they are going to spend the last few days of their honeymoon. In the car, Nina shuts her eyes and tries to sleep when all of a sudden

Philip brakes and she is thrown against the dashboard. They have hit something.

Oh, my God. A child! Nina cries.

A pig has run across the road before Philip can stop. His back broken, the pig lies in the middle of the road, squealing. Each time he squeals, dark blood fills his mouth. Within minutes and seemingly from out of nowhere, men, women, and children have gathered by the side of the road and are watching. Philip and Nina get out of the car and stand together. It is very hot and bright.

Putting her hand to her head to shade her eyes, she says, Philip, do something. The pig sounds just like a baby.

What do you want me to do? Philip answers. His voice is unnaturally shrill. Kill it?

A man wearing a straw hat approaches Philip. The man is carrying a stick. Philip takes his wallet out of his back pocket and, without a word, gives him twenty dollars. The man takes the twenty dollars and, likewise, does not say a word to Philip.

Back in the car, Nina and Philip do not speak to each other until they have reached Puerto Vallarta and until Nina says, Look there's the sea.

Then, he tells her about Iris.

An accident.

In bed that night, Philip says, I wonder if the guy in the hat carrying the stick was really the pig's owner. He could have been anyone.

Yes, Nina agrees. He could have been anyone.

These flea bites, she also says, are driving me crazy.

Me, too, Philip says, taking her in his arms.

* * *

She believes Philip loved her but how can she be certain of this? Knowledge is the goal of belief. But how can she justify her belief? Through logical proof? Through axioms that are known some other way, and by, for instance, intuition. Who thought of this? Socrates? Plato? She does not remember; she only remembers the name of her high school philosophy teacher, Mlle. Pieters, who was Flemish, and the way she said *Platoe*.

She should reread Plato. Plato might comfort her. Wisdom. Philosophy. Or study the Eastern philosophers. Zen. Perhaps she should become a Buddhist nun. Shave her head, wear a white robe, wear cheap plastic sandals.

She hears the wind outside shake the branches of the trees. Again, the shutter bangs against the side of the house. Now who will fix it?

Who will mow the lawn? Who will change the lightbulb in the hall downstairs that she cannot reach? Who will help her bring in the groceries?

How can she think of these things?

She is glad it is night and the room is dark.

Time is much kinder at night—she has read this somewhere recently.

If she was to turn and look at the clock on the bedside table, she would know the time—ten, eleven, twelve o'clock or already the next day? But she does not want to look. Instead, if she could, she would reverse the time. Have it be yesterday, last week, years ago.

In Paris, in a café on the corner of boulevard Saint-Germain and rue du Bac. She can picture it exactly. It is not yet spring, still cold, but already the tables are out on the sidewalk so that the pedestrians have to step out into the street. It is Saturday and crowded. The chestnut trees have not yet begun to bloom, a few green shoots on the branches give out a hopeful sign.

She remembers what she is wearing. A man's leather bomber jacket she has bought secondhand at an outdoor flea market, a yellow silk scarf, boots. At the time, she thinks she looks French and chic. Perhaps she does. In any event, he thinks she is French.

Vous permettez? he asks, pointing to the empty chair at her table.

She is drinking a *café crème* and reading a French book, *Tropismes* by Nathalie Sarraute.

Je vous en prie, she says, without looking up at him.

She works at an art gallery a few blocks away on rue Jacques-Callot. The gallery primarily shows avant-garde American painters. The French like them and buy their work. Presently, the gallery is exhibiting a Californian artist whose work she admires. The artist is older, well-known, wealthy; he has invited Nina to the *hôtel particulier* on the Right Bank where he is staying. He has told her to bring her bathing suit—she remembers it still: a blue-and-white checked cotton two-piece. The pool is located on the top floor of the *hôtel particulier* and is paneled in dark wood, like one in an old-fashioned ocean liner; instead of windows there are portholes. She follows the artist into the pool and as she swims, she looks out onto the Paris rooftops and since night is falling, watches the lights come on. Floating on her back, she also watches the beam at the top of the Eiffel Tower protectively circle the city. Afterward, they put on thick white robes and sit side by side on chaise longues as if they are, in fact, on board a ship, crossing the Atlantic. They even drink something—a Kir royal. She slept with him once more but they did not go swimming again. Before he leaves Paris, he gives her one of his drawings, a small cartoonlike pastel of a ship, its prow shaped like the head of a dog. Framed, the drawing hangs downstairs in the front hall.

Philip begins by speaking to her about Nathalie Sarraute. He claims to know a member of her family who is distantly related to him by marriage.

At the time, she does not believe him.

A line, she thinks.

She hears the phone ring downstairs. As a precaution, she has turned it off in the bedroom—why, she wonders? So as not to wake him? She reaches for the receiver but the phone abruptly stops midring. Just as well. She will wait until morning. In the morning she will make telephone calls, she will write e-mails, make arrangements; the death certificate, the funeral home, the church service—whatever needs to be done. Tonight—tonight, she wants nothing.

She wants to be alone.

Alone with Philip.

*   *   *

She is not religious.

She does not believe in an afterlife, in the transmigration of souls, in reincarnation, in any of it.

But he does.

I don't believe in reincarnation and that other stuff and I don't go to church but I do believe in a God, he tells her.

Where were they then?

Walking hand in hand along the quays at night, they stop a moment to look across at Notre-Dame.

Mathematicians, I thought, weren't supposed to believe in God, she says.

Mathematicians don't necessarily rule out the idea of God, Philip answers. And, for some, the idea of God may be more abstract than the conventional God of Christianity.

At her feet, the river runs black and fast, and she shivers a little inside her leather bomber jacket.

Like Pascal, Philip continues, I believe it is safer to believe that God exists than to believe He does not exist. Heads God exists and I win and go to heaven, Philip motions with his arm as if tossing a coin up in the air, tails God does not exist and I lose nothing.

It's a bet, she says, frowning. Your belief is based on the wrong reasons and not on genuine faith.

Not at all, Philip answers, my belief is based on the fact that reason is useless for determining whether there is a God. Otherwise, the bet would be off.

Then, leaning down, he kisses her.

*   *   *

His eyes shut, Philip lies on his back. His head rests on the pillow and she has pulled the red-and-white diamond-patterned quilt up to cover him. He could be sleeping. The room is tidy and familiar, dominated by the carved mahogany four-poster. Opposite it, two chairs, her beige cashmere sweater hanging on the back of one; in between the chairs stands a maple bureau whose top is covered with a row of family photos in silver frames—Louise as a baby, Louise, age nine or ten, as the Black Swan in her school production of *Swan Lake,* Louise holding her dog, Mix, Louise dressed in a cap and gown, Louise and Philip sailing, Louise, Philip, and Nina horseback riding at a dude ranch in Montana, Louise and Nina skiing in Utah. Also on top of the bureau is a lacquer box where she keeps some of her jewelry. Her valuable jewelry—a diamond pin in the shape of a flower, a three-strand pearl necklace, a ruby signet ring—is inside the combination safe in the hall closet. Closing her eyes, she tries to remember the combination: three turns to the left to 17, two turns to the right to 4, and one turn to the left to 11 or is it the other way around? In any case she can never get the safe open; Philip has to. And, next to the lacquer jewelry box, the blue-and-green clay bowl Louise made for them in third grade in which, each evening, Philip places his loose change. The closet doors are shut and only the bathroom door is ajar.

When is a door not a door? When it is a . . .

Stop.

Perhaps she should put on her nightgown and lie down next to him and in the morning, when he wakes up he will reach for her the way he does. He will hike up her nightgown. Take it off, he will say. He likes to make love in the morning. Sleepy, she takes longer to respond.

She has not bothered to draw the curtains. Outside, above the waving tree branches, she can make out a few stars in the night sky. A mere dozen in a galaxy of a billion or a trillion stars. Perhaps death, she thinks, is like one of those stars—a star that can be seen only backward in time and exists in an unobservable state. While life, she has heard said, was created from stars—the stars' debris.

What did he say to her exactly?

> I am a bit tired, I am going to lie down for a minute before supper.

or

> I am going to lie down for a minute before supper, I am a bit tired.

or something else entirely.

She is in the kitchen. Spinning the lettuce. She looks up briefly.

How was your day?

She half listens to his reply.

We had a faculty meeting. You should hear how those new physicists talk! They're crazy, Philip says, as he goes upstairs.

She makes the salad dressing, she sets the table. She takes the chicken out of the oven. She boils new potatoes. Then she calls him.

Philip! Dinner is ready.

She starts to open a bottle of red wine but the cork is stuck. He will fix it.

Again, Philip, Philip! Dinner!

Before she walks into the bedroom, she knows already.

She sees his stocking feet. He has taken off his shoes.

What was he thinking? About dinner? About her? A paper he is reading by one of his students, arguing that Kronecker was right to claim that the Aristotelian exclusion of completed infinites could be maintained?

Infinites. Infinite sets. Infinite series.

Infinity makes her anxious.

It gives her nightmares. As a child, she had a recurring dream. A dream she can never put into words. The closest she comes to describing the dream, she tells Philip, is to say that it has to do with numbers. The numbers—if in fact they are numbers—always start out small and manageable, although in the dream Nina knows that this is temporary, for soon they start to gather force and multiply; they become large and uncontrollable. They form an abyss. A black hole of numbers.

You're in good company, is what Philip tells her. The Greeks, Aristotle, Archimedes, Pascal all had it.

The dream?

No, what the dream stands for.

Which is?

The terror of the infinite.

But, for Philip, infinity is a demented concept.

Infinity, he says, is absurd.

* * *

"Suppose, one dark night," is how Philip always begins his undergraduate course on probability theory, "you are walking down an empty street and suddenly you see a man wearing a ski mask carrying a suitcase emerge from a jewelry store—the window of the jewelry store, you will have noticed, is smashed. You will no doubt assume that the man is a burglar and that he has just robbed the jewelry store but you may, of course, be dead wrong."

Philip is a popular teacher. His students like him. The women in particular, Nina cannot fail to notice.

He is so sanguine, so merry, so handsome.

Vous permettez?

He is so polite.

Too polite, she sometimes reproaches him.

They do not go to bed with each other right away. Instead he questions her about the well-known American painter.

I don't want you to sleep with anyone else but me, he says. He sounds quite fierce. They are standing on the corner of boulevard Saint-Germain and rue de Saint-Simon, near the apartment where he is staying with his widowed aunt. A French aunt—or nearly French. She married a Frenchman and has lived in France for forty years. Tante Thea is more French than the French. She talks about politics and about food; she is impeccably dressed and perfectly coiffed; she serves three-course lunches, plays golf at an exclusive club in Neuilly, goes to the country every weekend. She refers to Philip as *mon petit Philippe* and, over time, Nina grows to like her.

A hot Saturday afternoon, the apartment will be empty. Across the boulevard, a policeman stands guarding a ministry. A flag droops over the closed entryway. Cars go by, a bus, several noisy motorcycles. They stand together not saying a word.

Come, Philip finally says.

Mon petit Philippe.

Nina smiles to herself, remembering.

He is so tentative, so determined to please her.

"The assumption that the man in the ski mask has robbed the jewelry store is an example of plausible reasoning but we, in this class"—is how Philip continues his lecture—"will be studying deductive reasoning. We will look at how intuitive judgments are replaced by definite theorems—and that the man robbing the jewelry store is in fact the owner of the jewelry store and he is on his way to a costume party, therefore the ski mask, and the neighbor's kid has accidentally thrown a baseball through his store window.

"Any questions?"

Most probably a sudden cardiac arrest—not a heart attack—their neighbor, an endocrinologist, says. He tries to explain the difference to her. A heart attack is when a blockage in a blood vessel interrupts the flow of blood to the heart, while a cardiac arrest results from an abrupt loss of heart function. Most of the cardiac arrests that lead to sudden death occur when the electrical impulses in the heart become rapid or chaotic. This irregular heart rhythm causes the heart to suddenly stop beating. Some cardiac arrests are due to extreme slowing of the heart. This is called bradycardia.

Did he say all of that?

No, no, Philip has never been diagnosed with heart disease. Philip is as healthy as a horse. He had a physical a few months ago. That is what his doctor said. In any case it is what Philip told her his doctor said.

No, no, Philip does not take any medication.

Their neighbor, Hugh, looks for a pulse. He puts both hands on Philip's heart and applies pressure. He counts out loud—one, two, three, four—until thirty.

Nina tries to count out loud with him—nineteen, twenty, twenty-one . . .

She has trouble making a sound above a whisper.

Poor Hugh, he does not know what to say—something about a defibrillator only it is too late. His dinner napkin is still hanging from his belt and he only notices it now. Blushing slightly, he pulls it off.

No. He must not call anyone.

Nina ran next door to fetch him just as he and his wife, Nell, are sitting down to their supper in the kitchen. Their dog, an old yellow Lab, stands up and begins to bark at her; upstairs, a child starts to cry. They have two children, one a month old. A girl named Justine. A day or two after Nell came home from the hospital, Nina went over with a lasagna casserole and a pink sweater and matching cap for the baby. How long ago that seems.

Hugh says, Call us any time. Nell and I . . . His voice trails off.

Yes.

Yes, yes, I will.

And call your physician. He'll have to draw up the death certificate.

Yes, in the morning, I will.

Will you be all right . . . ? Again, his voice trails off.

Yes, yes. I want to be alone.

Thank you.

Thank you, she says again.

She hears the front door shut.

Bradycardia.

The name reminds her of a flower. A tall blue flower.

Iris.

An old-fashioned name.

The name of the woman killed in the car accident. She must have been pretty, Nina imagines. Slender, blonde. Both are young—Iris is only eighteen and he is driving her home after a party, it is raining hard—perhaps Philip has had one drink too many but he is not drunk. No. Around a curve, he loses control of the car—perhaps the car skids, he does not remember; nor did he when the police question him. They hit a telephone pole. Iris is killed instantly. He, on the other hand, is unhurt.

Nina wonders how often Philip still thinks about Iris. Did he think of her before he died? Did he think he might have had a happier life had he married her? In a way, Nina envies Iris. Iris has remained forever young and pretty in his mind while he has only to glance at her and see how Nina's skin is wrinkled, her hair, once auburn or red—depending on the light—is gray, her breasts have lost their firmness.

Philip spoke of the accident on their honeymoon, on their way to Puerto Vallarta.

I just want you to know that this happened to me is what he says.

It happened also to Iris is what Nina wants to say but does not.

It took me a long time to get over it and come to terms with it is what he also says.

How did you come to terms with it? Nina wants to ask.

It was a terrible thing.

Yes.

Now, I don't want to think about it anymore, he says.

And I don't want to talk about it anymore. Do you understand, Nina?

Nina said she does but she doesn't.

What was she like? Iris? she nonetheless asks. She tries to sound respectful. Was she Southern? Iris is such an unusual name.

She was a musician, Philip answers.

Oh. What did she play? The piano?

But Philip does not answer.

When she first arrived in Paris, at the airport, she sees a man, in the immigration line ahead of her, take off his wedding ring and pin it to the lining of his attaché case with a safety pin that he must keep there for that purpose.

What about your wife? she wants to shout.

Sometimes, in her mind, she accuses Philip of losing his wedding ring on purpose.

*   *   *

Her throat is dry; she finds it hard to swallow.

Downstairs, the lights are on. She goes to the hall closet, which is full of coats. Hers, his—a navy blue wool coat, a parka, a down jacket, a raincoat, an old windbreaker. The windbreaker must be twenty-five years old. She remembers how proud Philip was when he bought it. The windbreaker was bright yellow and on sale and, he claimed, would last him a lifetime. He is right. Now the windbreaker is faded, the collar and cuffs are frayed, without thinking about it, she takes it out of the closet and puts it on. Carefully, she zips it up. Her hands go to the pockets. Slips of paper—bills, a to-do list: *car inspection, call George about leak in basement, bank, pick up tickets for concert*. The list, she recognizes, is several months old; coins, paper clips, a ticket stub are in the other pocket.

She walks into the dining room. The chicken, the new potatoes, the salad are all on the table. Cold, waiting. Nina starts to pick up a dish to put it away and changes her mind. Tomorrow, she thinks. Tomorrow she will have plenty of time to put things away, to do the dishes, to do—she cannot think what. Instead, she takes the bottle of wine with the cork stuck inside it. Again, she tries to pull the cork out but can't. Damn, she says to herself. She goes to the kitchen and gets a knife. With the handle of the knife, she pushes the cork inside the bottle and pours herself a glass of wine.

Still holding the knife, a sharp kitchen knife, she makes a motion with it as if to slit her throat. Catching a glimpse of her reflection in the dining room mirror, she shakes her head.

What would Louise think?

Holding the glass of wine, she goes back upstairs.

* * *

Outside, the sound of a police car siren. From the bedroom window, she sees a blue light flash by in the dark, then rush past the house and disappear. She thinks of the car full of teenagers playing loud music and she imagines it smashed into a tree, the windshield bits of glittering glass as smoke rises from the hood and someone in the backseat screams.

Another siren. Another police car goes by.

Poor Iris, she says to Philip.

Again, the phone rings.

Louise.

Earlier, she left Louise a message. *Louise, darling, something has happened. Call me as soon as you can.*

Poor Louise.

Philip's darling.

A beautiful, lively, headstrong young woman who looks like him—tall, dark, with the same gray eyes. Nina must answer the phone.

Hello, she says, picking up the receiver in the bedroom. Louise?

Whoever it is hangs up.

A wrong number. In the dark, Nina looks for a caller ID on the phone but there is none.

She is relieved. She does not want to tell Louise.

It is three hours earlier in California, and Louise, she imagines, is having dinner. She is having dinner with a young man. A handsome young man whom she likes. Afterward, Louise will not pick up her messages, she will sleep with him.

For Louise, Philip is alive still.

Lucky Louise.

Nina takes a sip of wine, then, putting down the glass, reaches for his hand again. His hand is cold and she attempts to warm it by holding it between both of hers.

She loves Philip's hands. His long blunt fingers. Fingers that have touched her in all kinds of ways. Passionate ways about which she does not want to let herself think—making her come. She presses the hand to her lips.

When did they last make love?

A Sunday morning, a few weeks ago. The house is quiet, the curtains are drawn, and the bedroom is dark enough. She is self-conscious about being too old for sex. Also, it takes him longer.

In Paris, too, in Tante Thea's old-fashioned, shuttered apartment on the rue de Saint-Simon, where, on the way to Philip's bedroom, she bumps into furniture—side tables, spindly-legged chairs, glass cases filled with porcelain figurines—and where in bed, afterward, Philip admits that he was nervous. Without telling her why, he says he had not made love in a long time. He was afraid, he says, he had forgotten how.

You can never forget—like riding a bicycle, Nina adds.

This or her trite remark makes him laugh and, reassured or, at least, not as nervous, Philip makes love to her again.

* * *

Has he been faithful to her?

She reaches for the glass of wine.

Also, not thinking, Nina reaches into the windbreaker pocket and pulls out a coin. It feels like a penny.

Heads? Tails?

"The probability of an event occurring when there are only two possible outcomes is known as a binomial probability," Philip tells his students. "Tossing a coin, which is the simple way of settling an argument or deciding between two options, is the most common example of a binomial probability. Probabilities are written as numbers between one and zero. A probability of one means that the event is certain—"

When Louise is six years old, she begins to play a game of tossing pennies with Philip. She records the results along with the dates in a little orange notebook, which she keeps in the top drawer of Philip's bedside table:

> *5 heads, 10 tails — 10/10/1976*
> *9 heads, 11 tails — 3/5/1977*
> *17 heads, 13 tails — 2/9/1979*

The more times you toss a coin, Lulu, Philip tells Louise, the closer you get to the true theoretical average of heads and tails.

> *5039 heads, 4961 tails — 3/5/1987*

For the last entry, Louise relies on a calculator.

"Another thing to remember and most people have difficulty understanding this," Philip continues to tell his class as he takes a penny out of his pocket and tosses it up in the air, "is if a coin has come up heads a certain number of times, it will not necessarily come up tails next, as a corrective. A chance event is not influenced by the events that have gone before it. Each toss is an independent event."

Heads, Philip tells Louise.

Heads, again.

Heads.

Tails, he says.

Nina, on an impulse, throws the coin she found in the pocket of Philip's windbreaker up in the air. Too dark to see which way it comes up, she places the coin on top of the bedside table. In the morning she will remember to look:

Heads is success, tails is failure

And record the date in Louise's orange notebook: *5/5/2005. 5 5 5*

What, she wonders, do those three 5s signify?

Numbers are the most primitive manifestations of archetypes. They are found inherent in nature. Particles, such as quarks and protons, know how to count—how does she know this? By eating, sleeping, breathing next to Philip. Particles may not count the way we do but they count the way a primitive shepherd might—a shepherd who may not know how to count beyond three but who can tell instantly whether his flock of, say, 140 sheep, is complete or not.

Also, she remembers the example of the innumerate shepherd and his sheep.

She drinks a little more wine. She has not eaten since noon but chewing food seems like an impossible task. A task she might have performed long ago but has forgotten how.

She would like a cigarette. She has not smoked in twenty years yet the thought of lighting it—the delicious whiff of carbon from the struck match—and inhaling the smoke deep into her lungs is soothing. She and Philip both smoked once.

In Tante Thea's apartment, after making love for the first time, they share a cigarette, an unfiltered Gauloise. They hand it back and forth to each other as they lie on their backs, naked, on the lumpy single bed—the ashtray perched on her stomach. And later when they begin to kiss again, she remembers how Philip licks off a piece of cigarette paper stuck to her lip, and, then, how he swallows it. At the time, it seems a most intimate gesture.

As if she is exhaling smoke, Nina lets out a long deep breath.

Are you a spy? she asks. Are you employed by the CIA?

At the beginning, she makes a point to be difficult. She does not intend to be an easy conquest. She does not want to fall in love yet.

No. Yes. If that is what you want to believe.

Philip has a Fulbright scholarship and is teaching under-graduate math for a year at the École Polytechnique.

And do all the girls have a crush on you?

Alas, there aren't many girls in my class. The few are the grinds. Philip makes a face of distaste.

There's Mlle. Voiturier and Mlle. Epinay. They sit together and don't say a word. They have terrible B.O.

In spite of herself, Nina laughs.

Do I? Nina makes as if to smell her underarm.

No. What perfume do you wear?

L'Heure Bleue.

Philip smells faintly of ironed shirts.

He still does.

Spring. The weather is warm, the chestnut trees are in flower, brilliant tulips bloom in the Luxembourg Garden. In the evenings, they stroll along the quays bordering the darkening Seine, watching the tourist boats go by. On one such evening, a boat shines its light on them, illuminating them as they kiss. On board, everyone claps and Philip and Nina, only slightly embarrassed, wave back.

What I was saying about whether God exists or not, Philip continues as they resume walking hand in hand, is that, according to Pascal, we are forced to gamble that He exists.

I'm not forced to gamble, Nina says, and believing in God and trying to believe in Him are not the same thing.

Right but Pascal uses the notion of expected gain to argue that one should try to lead a pious life instead of a worldly one, because if God exists one will be rewarded with eternal life.

In other words, the bet is all about personal gain, Nina says.

Yes.

On the way home, as Nina crosses the Pont Neuf, the heel of her shoe catches, breaks off. She nearly falls.

Damn, she says, I've ruined my shoe.

Holding on to Philip's arm, she limps across the street.

A sign, she says.

A sign of what?

That I lead a worldly life.

Shaking his head, Philip laughs.

On a holiday weekend, they drive to the coast of Normandy. They walk the landing beaches and collect stones—in her studio, they are lined up on the windowsill along with stones from other beaches. At Colleville-sur-Mer, they make their respectful way among the rows and rows of tidy, white graves in the American cemetery.

How many?

9,387 dead.

On the way to La Cambe, the German military cemetery, it begins to rain.

Black Maltese crosses and simple dark stones with the names of the soldiers engraved on them mark the wet graves.

More than twice as many dead—according to the sign.

Why did we come here? Nina asks. And it's raining, she says.

Instead of answering, Philip points. Look, he says.

In the distance, to the west, there is clear sky and a faint rainbow.

Make a wish, Nina says.

I have, Philip answers.

Always, on their trips, they stay in cheap hotels—neither one of them has much money. Closing her eyes, she can still visualize the rooms with the worn and faded flowered wallpaper, the sagging double bed with its stiff cotton sheets and uncomfortable bolster pillows; often there is a sink in the room and Philip pees in it; the toilet and tub are down the hall or down another flight of stairs. Invariably, too, the rooms are on the top floor, under the eaves, and if Philip stands up too quickly and forgets, he hits his head. The single window in the room looks out onto a courtyard with hanging laundry, a few pots of geranium, and a child's old bicycle left lying on its side. The hotels smell of either cabbage or cauliflower—*chou-fleur*.

Chou-fleur, she repeats to herself. She likes the sound of the word.

Always, in her mind, she and Philip are in bed.

Or they are eating.

During dinner at a local restaurant, over their *entrecôtes—saignante* for him, *à point* for her—their *frites*, and a carafe of red wine, Philip talks about his class at the École Polytechnique, about what he is teaching—*nombres premiers, nombres parfaits, nombres amiables.*

Tell me what they are, she says, in between mouthfuls. She is always hungry. Starving, nearly.

I've told you already, he says, pouring her some wine. You weren't listening.

Tell me again about the ones I like, the amiable ones.

Amiable numbers are a pair of numbers where the sum of the proper divisors of one number is equal to the other. 220 and 284 are the smallest pair of amiable numbers and the proper divisors of 220 are—Philip shuts his eyes—1, 2, 4, 5, 10, 11, 20, 22, 44, 55, and 110, which add up to 284, and the proper divisors of 284 are 1, 2, 4, 71, and 142, which add up to 220—do you see?

Imagine figuring that out, she says, waving a forkful of *frites* in the air.

Who did?

Thābit ibn Qurrah, a ninth-century Arab mathematician.

How many amiable numbers are there?

No one knows.

Then there are the perfect numbers—6 is a perfect number. The divisors of 6 are 1, 2, and 3, which add up to 6.

But she has stopped listening to him. Perfection interests her less.

Do you want dessert? she asks. The *crème caramel* or the *tarte aux poires*?

She talks to him about how, more than anything, she wants to paint. Paint like her favorite artist, Richard Diebenkorn.

His still life and figure drawings. Do you know his work?

Philip shakes his head.

I'll show them to you one day.

They argue, but without rancor, discussing and exchanging ideas. Both are attracted by abstractions. Sometimes she forgets that she has not known Philip all her life or not known him for years.

It was a happy time and they are married in the fall.

* * *

More than 10 percent of a person's daily thought is about the future, or so she has heard say. Out of an average of eight hours a day, a person spends at least one hour thinking about things that have not yet happened. This will not be true for her. She has no desire to think about the future. For her, the future does not exist; it is an absurd concept.

She prefers to think about the past. Yesterday, for instance? She tries to remember what she and Philip did yesterday. What they said. What they ate.

When did she last speak to Louise? On the telephone, Louise described her job with the Internet start-up—a promotion, a raise, a cause for celebration. And is she, at this very moment, celebrating at her favorite Japanese restaurant? Nina pictures Louise talking excitedly to the young man who sits across from her, and as deftly with her chopsticks, she picks up expensive raw fish and puts it in her mouth.

Three weeks before her due date, alone—Philip is at a conference in Miami—in the third-floor walk-up apartment in Somerville, Nina wakes up with contractions. Hastily, she gets dressed, collects a few things, and calls a taxi. The taxi company does not answer. She tries to time the contractions but she barely has time to recover from one before she has another. Again she tries to call the taxi company, again she gets no answer. She dials 911. For the first time, she notices that it is snowing. Snow swirls in great wind-driven whorls blanketing the parked cars, the trees, obscuring the street. Putting on her coat and picking up her bag, she starts downstairs; once her foot catches and she trips, falling down several steps. In an apartment below, a dog begins to bark and she hears someone shout, *Shut up, damn it.* Half afraid whoever it is will come out and find her, she holds her breath. In the front hall of their building, her water breaks, a stream hitting the cracked linoleum floor. A few moments later, she sees a car pull up and, muffled in a hat and coat, a policeman runs to the door. Rosy-faced from the cold, he looks young—younger than she. Leading her out into the snow, he holds Nina up under the arms to keep her from slipping in her flimsy leather moccasins—the only shoes that still fit, so swollen has all of her become—as they make their way to the car.

She lies down in the back of the police car, a grille separating her, like a criminal, from the back of the head and shoulders of the young policeman who is driving. The streets are unplowed and covered in several inches of new snow and she is aware of the eerie reflection of the car's blue light, illuminating her in surreal-like flashes. The policeman speaks to someone on his radio; *ten-four,* he repeats, as he drives; when he has to use the brake, the car skids sideways. A truck with chains rumbles noisily past them in the opposite direction and Nina, momentarily caught in the truck's headlights, has a glimpse of the driver's surprised stare. Louise is almost there.

What, she wonders, does the young man in the restaurant with Louise look like?

Does he look like Philip?

* * *

Philip has an eidetic memory. He has total recall of names, places, and nearly every meal he has eaten—the good ones, in particular. He can quote entire passages from books and recite poems by heart: *The Rime of the Ancient Mariner*; *Paradise Lost*; Shakespeare's speeches: Now is the winter of our discontent / Made glorious summer by this son of York—she hears his voice taking on a sonorous tone along with a British accent. He can recite lengthy bits in Latin that he learned as a young boy.

A trick, he claims. One has to make an association between the words and a visual image that one positions in space. The Greeks knew how to do this. The story of Simonides is the classic example.

You told me once but I've forgotten it, Nina says.

Simonides was hired to recite a poem at a banquet but when he finished, his host, a nobleman, refused to pay him as he had promised, complaining that instead of praising him in the poem, Simonides praised Castor and Pollux and he should ask the two gods to pay him. Simonides was then told that two men were waiting for him outside and he left the banquet hall but when he got outside—

I remember now, Nina says. No one was there but the roof of the banquet hall collapsed, killing everyone. The corpses of the guests were so mangled that they were unrecognizable but since Simonides had a visual memory of where each had been sitting, he could identify them. I remember you told me that story on Belle-Île, one summer. We were in a café next to the harbor. I think we were waiting for the ferry and for Louise.

That's my point exactly, Philip says, smiling.

* * *

Closing her eyes, she can see the house on Belle-Île. A color-ful, old house, one side is painted red; the shutters, too, are red, a deeper, darker red. The plaster walls are a foot thick and the ceilings are low. Blue hydrangeas grow in dense hedges all around the house.

The house looks like the French flag, Philip says.

From Quiberon, they take the ferry. Often the sea is rough and the boat pitches and rolls, sending spray high up to splash the cabin windows where the passengers sit, blotting out the island as it grows closer. One time, Nina watches a farmer try to drive his horse and wagon on the boat and the horse, his hooves clattering noisily and drawing sparks, refuses at first to step onto the metal ramp. It is low tide and the grade is steep and the horse rears and nearly breaks his harness. He is a big white farm horse and during the entire voyage to Belle-Île, Nina hears him whinnying from below deck.

For close to twenty years, they rent the same house. The house belongs to a local couple, who slowly, slowly, over the years, renovate and modernize it, so that each summer there is something new—a stove, a fridge, an indoor toilet, curtains. Even in bad weather when they are forced to stay indoors, it makes little difference to Philip and Nina. Life on the island is simple, food is plentiful: oysters, langouste, all kinds of fish; every morning, in town, there is a market. Nina buys vegetables, bread, the local cheese—a goat cheese, with an acrid gamy taste. She and Philip swim, sit in the sun, read; one summer they read all of Proust in French: *Longtemps, je me suis couché de bonne heure. Parfois, à peine ma bougie éteinte, mes yeux se fermaient si vite que je n'avais pas le temps de me dire "Je m'endors."*—Philip can recite several more pages by heart. In the afternoon when the wind picks up, he goes sailing and she paints—or tries to.

Claude Monet, famously, spent a summer on Belle-Île. A framed poster of his painting of rocks off the Atlantic coast—rocks that look like prehistoric beasts sticking their pointed, dangerous heads out of the water—hangs in her studio. She has stared long and hard at both the painting and the rocks, which she, too, wants to paint. The sea, in particular. How menacing it looks in Monet's painting and how tame and lifeless in her own. Her sea looks like soup. Eventually, she gives up and destroys it. Later, back home, she paints the same scene abstractedly. The rocks are vertical brown lines, the sea blue, green, and red horizontal stripes. The painting is almost successful.

Louise learns how to swim and ride a two-wheel bicycle on Belle-Île. A few years later, Philip teaches her how to sail.

You should see how Lulu sets the spinnaker, Philip boasts. It takes her twenty seconds. He is proud of her.

Nina has an affair on Belle-Île but she does not want to think of that.

No, not now.

The house is only a short walk from the sea. The first thing she does when she arrives each summer is to go down to the beach and swim. The cold water is a shock, but bracing, and, after the long trip, it makes Nina feel clean.

*   *   *

Jean-Marc.

Is this the first time you've crossed the Atlantic? Nina asks, when she meets him.

Solo, he has sailed in a race from Belle-Île to an island in the Caribbean, and he has won. A celebration of his victory is being held at a local restaurant.

Fair-haired, solidly built, and not tall—no taller than Nina—his eyes are a light blue, like a dog's. A husky. Or the blue of the Caribbean. He is a bit younger than Nina.

No, no, he laughs at her. This is my ninth trip across the Atlantic.

Oh. Embarrassed, she turns away.

Standing beside him, his pretty wife, Martine, smiles up at him.

Next, Philip is asking Jean-Marc a lot of questions: What type of sails? Does he have radar? Loran? How accurate is it? Loran, she hears Philip say, suffers from the ionospheric effects of sunrise and sunset and is unreliable at night.

Navigation systems never posed a problem for me. But nature, yes, Jean-Marc answers. Nature can pose big problems. Two years ago, when I was halfway across the Atlantic, a whale attached herself to my boat. First she swam on one side of my boat, then she dove under and disappeared for a few minutes— Jean-Marc makes the motion of a whale diving with his hands— before she reappears again on the other side of my boat. She was playing with me. She continues like this for two days and two nights—I can still see the whale's little eyes shining up at me in the dark, Jean-Marc says, shaking his head. It makes me—how you say?—*complètement fou.*

In French, whale is feminine, *la baleine*, Philip explains to Nina, imitating Jean-Marc's accent and gestures, as he retells the story.

I know, she says.

Je sais.

Philip's assurance always astonishes her. It is not arrogance but a confidence, based in part on old-fashioned principles and in part on intelligence, that he is right and, usually, he is. For Nina, this is both a comfort and an irritant.

Strange, too, Nina reflects for perhaps the hundredth time, how Philip, who was born and raised hundreds of miles from the sea, should have become such a keen sailor. None of his family are.

It began with rowing on the Charles, he tells Nina. Then, one day, over Memorial Day weekend, my roommate took me out sailing on his family's boat, a thirty-three-foot ketch called the *Mistral*—I didn't know the difference between port and starboard—and we sailed over to Martha's Vineyard. The wind was just right, and I will never forget how peaceful I felt that night, lying on the deck and looking up at the stars and listening to the sound of the water against the boat's hull. In a funny way, it was a moment—how to describe it—where I felt completely at one. At one with the world and with the universe.

Maybe you got enlightened, Nina tells him.

Not very likely, Philip answers.

Right then and there I almost changed my major from math to astronomy and I also vowed to myself that one day I, too, would own a boat.

Downstairs in the basement, there is a decrepit rowing machine and, for years now, Nina has rarely heard the whirr of it. She has begun a campaign to throw the machine out. Useless outmoded junk, she claims. A fire hazard.

Now she can throw it out.

She takes a quick, almost furtive look out the window. The night seems very dark and silent. She can no longer see any stars. What is the saying Philip likes to quote? *I much prefer a bold astronomer to a decorous star.* She disagrees. She prefers a star to an invention.

It must be late, she decides.

She needs to get more wine. This time she will bring the bottle back upstairs.

He won't mind, she thinks.

"In general," Philip might say, were he to turn her infidelity into a classroom exercise, "if we know for certain that my wife is not having an affair, the probability of the event would be 0; but, should we discover that she is having an affair, the probability would be 1. The numerical measure of probability can range from 0 to 1—from impossibility to certainty. Thus, the probability of my wife being unfaithful would be 1 over 2 because there are only the two possibilities: that she is having an affair or that she is not having an affair."

While she and Jean-Marc are in bed one afternoon, some-one knocks at the front door and calls out Nina's name—the landlady checking on the new refrigerator or leaving her some fresh lettuce from her garden.

Un moment, Nina calls back down. *J'arrive.*

Only half dressed and holding his shoes in one hand, Jean-Marc climbs out the bedroom window. Jumping, he lands squarely on his feet. In another moment, he leaps over the hydrangea hedge and is gone.

Jean-Marc has the tight, muscular body of a gymnast.

"But let us take another example," Philip continues. "The probability of a person crossing a street safely is also 1 over 2 because again there are only two possible outcomes: crossing safely and not crossing safely. Yet the trouble with this argument is that the two possible outcomes—crossing safely and getting run over—are not equally likely. If they were, people would not want to cross the street very often or if they did, a lot of them would get hurt or killed. So therein lies the fallacy. The definition given by Fermat and Pascal applies only if one can analyze the situation into equally likely possible outcomes, which takes me back to my original example—and to put your minds at ease"—a few of the students laugh—"since I know my wife to be a truth-ful and loving woman, she is not likely to be unfaithful and to have had an affair."

General laughter and applause.

Trust is a word we have put too much trust in, Philip also tells his class.

* * *

Iris again.

Was Iris, like Philip, a native of Wisconsin? A blonde beauty of Scandinavian origin—her hair so blonde it is white. And a musical prodigy. Nina has read about children who learn how to play the piano at age three, compose their first piece at five, debut as a soloist at seven—was Iris one of them? She pictures her sitting, small and demure, a bow in her hair, on the piano bench in front of the Steinway grand, her feet reaching for the pedals as she starts to play. Her little hands move swiftly and assuredly; the sound she makes is passionate. She plays Philip's favorite Chopin polonaise—Nina can hear the melody in her head—which promises redemption and celebrates Polish heroism. Were they high school sweethearts and did they sleep together? Perhaps Iris is pregnant and she has just found out. Twice she has missed her period and every morning now she throws up her breakfast. She has screwed up her courage to tell Philip in the car on the way home from the party. The reason he drives off the road.

Nina leans over Philip. Lightly, she touches his cheek. How can this have happened? How can this be?

Philip is so robust, so healthy, so—she tries to think of the right words—so engaged in life.

Come back, she whispers. Please, come back.

How can he leave her?

Without saying good-bye.

Without a word.

Please, she pleads.

Putting her head down on his chest, she listens.

*   *   *

At home, some evenings, Philip likes to play music and take her in his arms and whirl her in a quick two-step to *La vie en rose*, down the front hall, past the umbrella stand, the closet full of coats and past the pastel of a ship, its prow shaped like the head of a dog.

The top of her head reaches his collarbone, she can feel his heart beating.

His shoes are on the floor next to the bed. Old-fashioned, scuffed-up, lace-up brown oxfords. One shoe is lying on its side. Abandoned. Should she pick up the shoes and put them away in the closet? No, she will leave them there.

She picks up after Philip. It annoys her—no, worse: it angers her. His socks, his underwear, left lying around for her to put away, to hang up, to throw in the laundry basket. At first, she scolds but then bored by her own aggrieved tone and the futility of her words, she stops.

Untidiness in a man, she has read somewhere, is a sign of his having had a mother who dotes and spoils her son. Not so, in Philip's case.

*   *   *

Alice, Philip's mother, lives twenty miles away in a nursing home. The last time Nina and Philip visit her, Alice is not certain who they are. Unfailingly polite, she speaks about people Nina has never heard of: Rick who built a fireplace made out of bricks—Rick rhymes with brick—nonsense. Nina lets her mind wander. She has brought tulips from the garden, which pleases Philip's mother.

I've always loved bougainvillea, she tells Nina.

Tulips, Mother, Philip tries to correct her. Tulips from our garden.

Francis, my husband, loved bougainvillea, Alice continues. Our garden in Ouro Prêto was full of bougainvillea.

Ouro Prêto? Where is that? Nina asks, paying more attention.

In Brazil, Philip answers. I've told you how the year after they got married, before Harold and I were born, she and my father spent a year in Brazil. Ouro Prêto was a mining town, originally, it means black gold. Now, there's a university. It's full of ornate, baroque churches—I've seen the photos they took. My father was doing some kind of research there. Afterward, they spent a year in Mexico.

Strange what she remembers, Philip also says.

How did you like living in Ouro Prêto? Nina leans forward to ask Alice. She feels a surge of tenderness for the old lady, who is sitting in her wheelchair dressed in a faded blue robe and whose pale, lined face has suddenly come to life.

Oh, yes, Alice says. I remember how every evening after Francis finished his work, we walked through town up into the hills where we could see all of Ouro Prêto spread out below us. We could see the gold spires of the churches glittering in the setting sun. I remember we had a little dog. She smiles. His name was Kilo.

What kind of dog? Nina asks. She wants Alice to remember.

A little dog we found in the street. He was black and brown. And white, Alice adds before she closes her eyes.

It's hard to imagine your mother as a young woman in Ouro Prêto, Nina says on the way home in the car.

But she can, easily.

Alice in a full skirt and an embroidered peasant blouse; she is wearing sandals; her dark hair reaches her waist. Hand in hand, she walks with Francis on the town's cobblestoned streets, the dog straining at the leash. When they reach the hills above the town, they sit for a moment under a tree. Perhaps they make love, Francis lifting Alice's full skirt while Kilo barks excitedly around them. Only it is hard to picture Francis, a formal, courtly man, having sex.

What are you smiling about? Turning to look at her, Philip asks.

Nothing.

Why, she wonders to herself, does she always have to picture people having sex?

Philip rarely speaks about his parents. Not from any resentment but from a sort of *pudeur*—a reticence. His parents, too, were reticent and undemonstrative. They hardly ever raised their voices, they rarely got angry. In their presence, Nina always felt too loud and flashy, too frivolous, although she is none of those things really.

Francis, Philip's father, taught anthropology; like Philip he was tall and slender, but he had a thick white mustache that hid his top lip. For a few months, while they lived in Berkeley, Philip grew a mustache.

* * *

I'm curious. I just want to see how it feels. Don't worry, I'll shave it off soon, he promises Nina. Only he doesn't.

It feels strange when you kiss me. And food gets stuck in it, it's unhygienic, Nina says.

She believes he has grown the mustache to annoy her.

Also, he has gotten into the habit of stroking it.

It makes you look weird, is what Louise says to him, and it embarrasses me in front of my friends. It is she, not Nina, who persuades Philip to shave it off.

What will she tell Alice now?

Nina tries to remember how long ago Philip's brother died. Five, six years, maybe seven. She has lost track. Poor Harold. Short, jovial, the son of the milkman, he joked behind his father's back. Harold married and divorced the same woman twice, which further subjected him to ridicule.

How often does that happen? Nina wonders.

More often than you think, Philip says.

You have to be an optimist.

Or an amnesiac.

Harold worked for an airline as a navigator, flying all over the country until he was fired. Harold drank too much and died of cirrhosis of the liver. At Philip and Nina's wedding, he passed out and Laura, one of her bridesmaids, found him lying on his back on the wet lawn, his fly open, his pecker out.

Nina pours herself more wine.

Most mathematical functions, Philip tells her, are classified as two-way functions because they are easy to do and easy to undo—take addition and subtraction, for example. The way turning a light on and turning it off is a two-way function. A one-way function is more complicated because, although it may be easy to do, you cannot undo it. Like mixing paint, you can't unmix it, or like breaking an egg shell, you can't put the egg back together again.

Like opening a bottle of champagne—for once Nina is listening—you can't put the cork back in the bottle. Or having a baby.

On account of the snowstorm, Philip's flight from Miami is canceled. He has to wait several hours before the runways at Logan Airport are cleared and he can come home.

I was frantic. I couldn't sit still or read, he tells Nina, when, breathless, his coat buttoned up the wrong way, he arrives at the hospital. I knew you were both fine but I wanted to be with you. I wanted to see her right away.

He is holding day-old Louise in his arms. There are tears in his eyes.

She touches Philip's cheek—cooler now. With her fingers, she traces the slightly raised scar on his forehead; she touches the lobe of his ear, his neck, his shoulders. Again she puts her head on his chest. He is all there still. But what, she wonders, happens when people die in cataclysmic ways, in explosions or in plane crashes, and their bodies disappear entirely or become ash, spindrift—a word she has always liked—or, simply, atoms? Are they still dead people? This leads her into the difficult realm of metaphysics. A realm she does not dare enter.

What about Philip's soul? Has his soul departed and is it now floating somewhere in the ether looking for a place to settle?

Outside, the wind arrives in strong gusts and she hears the tree branches shake; the shutter bangs again. Twice in quick succession.

Several afternoons a week, Philip goes sailing with Jean-Marc. Jean-Marc is good company, intelligent, serious, Philip tells Nina. He plans to open a sailing school on Belle-Île and Philip gives him business advice. In return, Jean-Marc is teaching Philip a great deal—not only about sailing but about the sea, the tides, the region.

You'll have to come with us, Philip tells Nina. I'll pick a good day, a day that isn't too windy. You'll like it, I promise. And, with Jean-Marc on board, you'll feel safe, he adds.

Yes, maybe, Nina, not yet keen on sailing, answers.

But she prefers to stay home, to read, sunbathe, swim. Sometimes she works a little in the garden, trimming the hydrangeas. Also, that summer she has begun to paint watercolors. She tries to do them fast; she wants to not hesitate.

How does it start?

They are having dinner at La Mère Irène, a popular restaurant, in Sauzon. The dinner is noisy, lively. Jean-Marc is a local son, a hero of sorts, he knows everyone—the chef, the waitresses, the other diners. They shout across the tables to one another; the food is local and cheap. Everyone drinks a lot of wine.

Philip is explaining Zeno's paradox. She no longer remembers why or how the subject came up, but she remembers that she is wearing a backless sundress with a red zigzag pattern that ties at the neck and she has thrown a white cotton sweater over her shoulders; she is eating *moules,* cooked in garlic and white wine, and *frites.*

This suggests that I can never cross a space, Philip says, holding up his glass of wine and pointing to the far side of the restaurant—he is sounding a little drunk—because I would have to pass an infinite number of points before I reach it. This also means that I would not be able to move any distance at all and motion itself would be impossible. Yet, of course, I can move, he almost shouts, which is why I believe that infinity, although an elegant and important concept in mathematics, does not hold up in the physical world. I don't know of any simple resolution to Zeno's paradox, but I know that I can walk across this room.

To demonstrate, Philip jumps up from his chair. Knocking it over, he trips and when he tries to stand on one leg—the leg that did not set properly—he loses his balance. He falls heavily, cutting his forehead on his wineglass.

Martine begins to cry.

Head wounds bleed a lot, Philip says, holding first one dinner napkin to his head, then another.

Jean-Marc accompanies them to the small clinic in Le Palais and stays while the attending doctor removes the imbedded shards of glass then stitches up Philip's head. The doctor insists that Philip spend the night in the clinic so that he can be observed, although he assures Nina that the risk of a concussion is slim.

Merely a precaution, he says.

Jean-Marc drives her home.

There are, she notices, bloodstains on the front of her back-less sundress. She also worries about her breath—that her breath smells of garlic. Also, too late, she realizes that the white cotton sweater must have slipped off her shoulders and, now, lies forgotten on the floor of La Mère Irène.

Zeno, Jean-Marc says, laughing and shaking his head, and untying her backless sundress.

Where, she tries to think, was Louise that summer?

It must have been the same summer Louise begs Philip and Nina to let her go to a girl's camp in New Hampshire.

What about Belle-Île? What about our sailing together? Philip is reluctant to let her.

All my friends are going to camp. Why can't I?

I'm not going to France. I hate France, Louise also says.

Look, I'll tell you what, Lulu. We'll toss a coin. Heads you go to camp, tails you go to France.

That's not fair.

Why?

Dad, please.

In tears, Louise runs out of the room.

Tossing a coin high up in the air, Philip slaps it down on the back of his hand. Heads, he shouts out to Louise. Heads, Lulu—you go to camp.

Let me see, Nina says.

It's tails.

* * *

Shivering, she hugs herself. The feel of the windbreaker's rough texture is a slight comfort. She can still hear the wind blowing outside and the room is quite dark.

In bed, Philip is an outline.

Go back, she tells herself. Go back.

She can feel his arms around her. His warm breath on her neck. Sweet, teasing, familiar. They have a good time together. They laugh a lot. Is laughter the secret to a good marriage, she wonders?

They know each other well.

Just what I was thinking, she says.

You read my mind, Philip says.

Is it the food they eat? The air they breathe?

They nearly have the same dream once.

In bed, she knows what he likes, what pleases him; he knows what pleases her, what gives her an orgasm. It is not complicated; it is not kinky, not an embarrassment. At times, it is perhaps too predictable, but as they get older and their options lessen, it is a comfort. They are both grateful. They are both gratified.

It has begun to rain, a gentle rattle against the glass. She goes to the window and opens it. Leaning out, she lets the rain fall on her face. A light cleansing mist and she breathes deeply. She imagines the grass, the plants, the trees, growing taller, greener.

Briefly, she wonders whether her studio windows are shut. No matter. The three canvases she is working on are of sky and water. Hard to tell where the water ends and where the sky begins.

She uses a lot of white paint. White and yellow and some blue paint. Just a hint of blue. Both the sea and sky look like bolts of cloth thrown down at random. The paintings are to be a triptych.

A triptych?

How presumptuous.

Who does she think she is? Hans Memling? Francis Bacon?

Tomorrow, first thing, she will destroy the canvases.

A car drives slowly by, its headlights blurry in the rain. Reluctantly, she shuts the window and draws the curtains before she goes and sits next to him again.

He drives too fast. Often, he is distracted.

Look over there, he says, one hand on the wheel, the other pointing.

A tree. A beautiful field.

Look out, she answers.

There's a car making a turn.

A truck.

Part of her feels—part of her even knows it for certain—that she, too, like Iris, will die in a car accident. It will be an awful coincidence. At the same time, isn't it true that events tend to duplicate one another? Like copycat murders. If there is a plane crash, instantly, there are two more.

"And what would be the probability of such a tragedy reoccurring?" he might later ask his class, as he writes out an equation on the blackboard. "The probability distribution of the number of occurrences of an event where n is the number of successes and N is the number of trials that happen rarely but have many opportunities to do so is called the Poisson distribution, named after a French mathematician, Siméon-Denis Poisson"—Philip stops to write the name on the blackboard—"and it is also known as the law of small or rare numbers, that Ladislaus von Bortkiewicz"—again, Philip turns to the blackboard to write out the name—"made famous when, in 1898, he published a book, *The Law of Small Numbers,* in which, during a period of twenty years, he recorded the number of soldiers kicked to death, each year, by horses in the fourteen Prussian cavalry corps. This is commonly known as the Prussian horse-kick data and it shows that the numbers follow a Poisson distribution."

She pictures it exactly. Rain coming down in dark sheets, the wipers straining, barely keeping the windshield clear, the road invisible, except for the unsteady red back lights of the car directly ahead. On either side of them, trucks leave huge splashing waves of water in their wakes, and, finally, the radio so full of static she turns it off.

We should get new windshield wipers, she says, in order to ease the tension she feels.

Philip does not answer. Hunched over in the driver's seat, for once, he is concentrating; next to him, she is in the passenger seat, the death seat.

Maybe we should pull over for a while, until the storm passes, she says.

Don't be silly, he answers.

"In fact," Philip adds in class, "many math historians feel that the Poisson distribution should have been renamed the

Bortkiewicz distribution. I don't have a strong opinion either way on the subject except that, frankly, I find Poisson a lot easier to spell."

Now, she will die some other way.

She pours herself more wine; the bottle is half empty

Every surface—the desk, the tables, the chairs, the windowsills—in his office downstairs and in his office in Cambridge is filled with stacks of papers, periodicals, journals. There are similar stacks all over the floor.

Philip rarely talks about his work—his work outside of his teaching—or if he does, he describes it as the art of counting without counting.

If Nina tries to describe it she says: the probabilistic methods in combinatorics.

Can you be a bit more specific, dear? Philip says, shaking his head and laughing at her.

No, I can't, Nina replies. Something to do with randomness.

Derandomization.

There you go, Philip says. You're getting warm.

Don't move anything, Philip warns Marta, the housekeeper. Don't touch anything.

No, no, Mr. Philip. I touch nothing, Marta replies, frowning. Her look conveys both disapproval and martyrdom.

Marta is from Colombia. Her two children, whom she has not seen in three years, live in a remote mountain village with her parents. Once a month, she sends the money she can spare back home to them.

Marta has worked for Nina for eight years. Nina trusts her completely. She gives Marta old clothes, leftover food, whatever she does not want. Every Wednesday morning at nine, she goes to pick up Marta at the bus stop and at three in the afternoon she drives her back.

What will she tell Marta on Wednesday?

A Catholic, Marta believes in God, in Jesus Christ, the Virgin Mary, in a whole bunch of saints. Marta will pray for Philip's eternal soul.

If only she could pray. But it is too late to believe in an omnipotent, omniscient, and benevolent God. And what would she pray for?

To be reunited with Philip in heaven? According to what she once read—she tries to remember where—the people on earth who have found the perfect spiritual and physical partner will be joined again in heaven for the rest of eternity in a union that—she now remembers where—Emanuel Swedenborg calls conjugial love.

And how did Swedenborg arrive at this belief?

Angels, he claimed, spoke to him.

Angels—Nina scoffs at the idea.

The bedroom curtains billow out in a sudden draft and startle her.

* * *

Again, she reaches for Philip's hand and, absently, she starts to twist the wedding ring around his finger—the ring they bought to replace the one he lost in the sea, off the coast of Brittany.

How did the silly story he told her go?

A fish, most probably, attracted by the shine of gold swallowed the ring, then, most probably, too, a bigger fish swallowed that fish, then a still bigger fish, a shark, swallowed the second fish and, who knows, Philip continues, my ring may finally have come to rest in an elegant restaurant in Shanghai or in Hong Kong. A surprise gleaming at the bottom of a bowl of shark fin soup.

When, years later, Philip is invited to a conference in Hong Kong, he comes back dazzled, dazzled by the sights and sounds and smells of China—nearly China.

The food as well.

At one of those floating restaurants in Aberdeen Harbor—a restaurant called Tai Pak—I got to pick the fish I wanted to eat out of a tank, he tells Nina, and, at the time, I couldn't help thinking about my wedding ring and wondering what my chances were of finding it inside the fish. A million to one? A billion to one?

But these things happen, Philip says. They happen more often than you think.

The fish I picked, he adds, was delicious.

He also attends an elegant dinner in someone's home on the Peak. The couple collects jade and the wife is Eurasian, he tells Nina. Her name is Sofia, like the city. Her father was born there, she confided to Philip during dinner. Her mother is Chinese. He drinks tea and eats tea cakes in the lobby of the Peninsula Hotel as the orchestra plays Strauss waltzes, he spends an afternoon at the horse races in Happy Valley, and goes shopping on Hollywood Road, where he buys Nina a red silk coat embroidered with green and blue peonies. An antique, but she rarely wears it. The coat smells of a too-sweet perfume—of tuberoses. It hangs in the back of her closet, its bright sheen hidden in plastic, so as not to eclipse her ordinary darker clothes.

Turn around, let me look at you, Philip says, when she first tries on the coat for him.

It fits you perfectly.

It was made to measure for you.

The color, too, suits you.

Sofia. She says the name outloud to herself.

Dr. Mayer, a therapist Nina went to for a year—the year she and Philip lived in Berkeley—tells her that jealousy sustains desire or that, at least, it arouses it, which also suggests how fragile desire is.

Dr. Mayer specializes in sex therapy. The walls of her office are covered with drawings of naked men and women coupling. She asks Nina a lot of intimate and embarrassing questions to which Nina replies with lies.

Not only do we need to find a partner, Dr. Mayer tells Nina, but we also need to find a rival.

She dislikes Dr. Mayer, she dislikes her self-assured tone, her taste in artwork, yet she feels duty bound to keep seeing her.

She tries to remember Dr. Mayer's first name. An unusual name. A name that does not suit her.

You cannot change the present but you can reinvent the past—did Dr. Mayer say this as well? Or did someone else?

What, she wonders, would she reinvent?

Philip did not know Iris. Iris is a stranger. Only as he is leaving the party—a graduation party from college—does he stop at the door and offer her a ride. She is standing alone—her friends have left without her. Also, it has begun to rain; lightning flashes in the sky followed by the not so distant sound of thunder. Perhaps he has noticed her earlier, perhaps they spoke briefly. Or he dances with her. He hardly remembers. She is wearing a pretty sleeveless dress with a pattern of some kind. Her arms are slender, and it turns out she lives a few blocks from Philip.

No problem, he says, I'll drive you home.

Thank you, I appreciate it, Iris says.

She does not have a coat. Gallantly, Philip takes off his jacket and puts it around her shoulders as they run to the car in the rain.

I've seen you around campus, he says, once they are inside his car.

I'm a freshman.

Oh.

What will you do next? Iris asks.

Go to graduate school. M.I.T.

Is that in Boston?

Cambridge, actually. And you? What do you want to do?

I don't know yet. Maybe teach. I like kids. There are seven of us in my family. She laughs when she tells Philip this.

Lucky you. I only have one brother.

Oh, yeah. Is he older or younger?

Boy, look at that rain come down, he might also have said.

Can you see all right? Since she does not drive herself, she is not overly concerned.

So what do you want to teach? Philip asks, turning to look at her with a smile.

They might have gone on talking like this until they reach her home. Polite conversation, small talk. She is pretty in a pale, fragile sort of way and Philip might have wondered whether he will try to kiss her when he drops her off and whether she will let him—except that around a sharp curve in the road, a truck going the other way takes the curve too wide and crosses the dividing line. To avoid hitting the truck, Philip drives off the road.

Iris holds out her slender arms as if to ward off a blow and she lets out a little scream, more like a yelp.

Unaware of what has occurred, the truck driver keeps on going in the blinding rain.

Philip has no memory of the near miss or of the truck.

Only, on occasion, on a predawn, dark morning, awakening, he again hears that yelp.

* * *

She and Philip have been married for forty-two years, six months, and how many days? How many hours?

How childish she is.

And during those forty-two years how many countries have they been to? How many houses have they lived in? How many animals have they owned?

The animals are for Louise.

Two dogs, a cat, a hamster, several goldfish.

Louise must have finished dinner by now, she thinks.

And, of course, in those forty-two years, how many times have they made love?

What is the old joke about the beans in the jar? A bean goes into a jar for each time a couple makes love during their first year of marriage, then a bean comes out of the jar for each time the couple makes love ever after.

Nina first has sex on a camping trip. Inside a tent, on a sleeping bag, she remembers the discomfort of it—a stone or a root digs into the small of her back—then the sharp pain of her hymen tearing. In his excitement, the boy, whose name is Andrew, comes right away. They are camped near a stream and, as soon as he rolls off her, she takes the flashlight and goes outside. Shining the light on the insides of her legs, she sees that they are smeared with blood and sperm. Barefoot, she walks into the stream. The stones hurt her feet but the water is so cold it numbs them. Squatting, she begins to wash, throwing the cold water up herself with her hands when, across the stream, she hears a thrashing noise.

Andrew, she calls.

The thrashing is louder.

A bear, she thinks. A bear attracted by the smell of blood.

Andrew, she calls again.

Sounds are magnified at night, Andrew tries to explain.

A squirrel or a rabbit, he guesses.

She tells the story to Philip, only she changes it. For some unacknowledged reason, she does not want Philip to know how or when she lost her virginity and how distasteful it was. Instead, she tells him how, unexpectedly, during the night, she gets her period and how, flashlight in hand, she goes to the stream to wash.

I've never run so fast, she says.

The probability of a bear—Philip starts to say, but Nina cuts him off.

Priscilla—she remembers, Dr. Mayer's first name.

For an instant, she wonders what has become of Andrew.

Doctor? Lawyer? Fireman?

She hardly remembers what he looks like—only that he was blond and robust—and chances are she would not recognize him—people change, age.

Sex with Philip is fine, she tells Dr. Mayer. They make love at least once a week. On Sunday morning, usually. And, yes, she always has an orgasm. The problem lies elsewhere. That part is partly true. Nina feels resentful, bored, unfulfilled—how many different ways are there to describe this? The truth is, she refuses to sleep with Philip on Sunday or on any other day. A way of punishing him— she is not sure for what—only she does not tell Dr. Mayer this.

Dr. Mayer suggests that Nina find something to do. Something that interests her and makes her feel useful. She, Dr. Mayer, for instance, goes to a hospice in Sausalito once a week. She counsels people who are dying.

Why don't you volunteer? she asks Nina. Volunteer at a homeless shelter.

For no reason she can explain, Nina starts to cry.

Dr. Mayer suggests that Nina and Philip come in together, as a couple.

The suggestion makes Nina cry harder.

Dr. Mayer suggests Nina take medication. Homeopathic medication.

Philip rarely takes anything—not even an aspirin after he falls and cuts his head in the restaurant on Belle-Île and when, the next day, the whole side of his face is black and blue.

What about when you fell out of the tree and broke your leg? Nina asks him. A compound fracture with the bone sticking out must have been very painful.

I guess it was. A stoic, Philip rarely complains.

How old were you then?

I'm not sure. Nine or ten.

* * *

Outside, the rain, heavy now, beats against the window pane.

The year they spend in Berkeley, it rains every day—thirty-four inches of precipitation in that year alone. Or dense fog. She hates the eucalyptus trees that line the street on which they live—how their bark hangs in long loose strips like flayed flesh. The rented house has a deck with a hot tub on it but she soon grows tired of sitting in it by herself. How old is Louise then? Eleven, twelve? She has to drive her everywhere: to school, to tennis lessons, to piano and ballet. Except on Saturdays, when Louise goes horseback riding and Philip drives her to the stables in Marin. He sits in the car and corrects student papers while he waits for her. Or else he goes to a nearby coffee shop and reads the newspaper. Lorna lives in Marin. Lorna, the brilliant, unstable, curly-haired Irish astrophysicist, who overdoses on sleeping pills.

Each morning, Nina takes the little white pills Dr. Mayer has prescribed. The pills look alike but are gold, silver, copper, and she lets them melt on her tongue. They are supposed to dispel her anxiety, her malaise.

Another nice word.

Chou-fleur, malaise—she will keep a list.

And, twice a week, she drives across the Bay Bridge to work in a battered-women's shelter in San Francisco. She works in the office, stuffing envelopes, licking and stamping them—mind-numbing work.

Away all day, in addition to teaching, Philip is doing research at the university. He is stimulated, satisfied, and exercised.

He rides home on his bicycle and they argue.

You said you would be home at seven. It's now after eight. Ten past eight.

I'm sorry. The meeting went on longer than I thought.

Dinner is ruined.

I said I was sorry.

Last night you said—

Nina, please don't start that up again.

Tell me why not?

Mom. Dad.

Okay, honey. Let's sit down and eat.

And Nina slams down the overcooked dish on the table, spilling some of its contents, and runs upstairs.

Mom!

Louise is thirty-five and not yet married.

Who will walk her down the aisle?

She takes another sip of wine.

Mon chéri, she leans over to whisper to him.

Ma chérie, is how he answers her.

So Louise won't understand, they occasionally speak French. They say things like *Un avion est tombé au milieu de l'Atlantique et il paraît que tous les passagers sont morts,* or *On dit que Jim le garagiste en ville a violé une petite fille,* but soon Louise understands enough French and asks, What plane crashed? Who died? or Jim did what?

Now they speak about more ordinary things; sometimes, she swears in French—*merde*, she says, if she accidentally bumps into something or if she drops a dish and it breaks.

Merde is also how one says "good luck" in French.

"Luck alone," Philip tells his students, "rarely solves a mathematical problem but concentration and imagination do. Especially the imagination." To prove his point, he tells the story of what the German mathematician David Hilbert is reported to have said when one of his students dropped out of his math class to become a poet: "Good—he did not have the imagination to become a mathematician."

"Any of you poets?" Philip asks.

For a few seconds lightning illuminates the room and Philip's face—his high brow, his deep-set eyes, his determined, chiseled chin.

Abe.

The nickname some of his colleagues have given him on account of his height and lanky frame; she rarely uses it.

He has also been mistaken for a Jew, but his grandparents were Polish Catholics from a town in Silesia.

One and two and three and four and five, Nina counts, waiting for the thunder, which sounds at number seven.

She is afraid of thunderstorms, of lightning striking the house, but tonight it will not matter.

She is not afraid.

* * *

A loud clap of thunder followed by a blue light filling the cabin of his boat is how Jean-Marc describes being struck by lightning to her. The acrid smell of ozone and burning electrical insulation, he adds, grimacing and reaching for her pack of cigarettes although he does not smoke.

She is sitting outside in a deck chair, sunbathing. She is topless.

She did not hear him arrive and it is too late to put the top of her bathing suit back on.

Overhead, dark clouds have begun to form and, in the garden, the hydrangeas have taken on a darker, almost navy blue hue. It is about to rain. The reason they talk about the weather and the possibility of an approaching storm.

He has brought over a book for Philip. A book on sailing.

Philip is out, she tells Jean-Marc. He's playing tennis.

Dieu merci, the sailboat was grounded, Jean-Marc continues, exhaling a stream of smoke, but the lightning destroys the radio, the radar, the Loran, the navigation lights, all the electronics on board. Fortunately, I was not far from shore.

How far? she asks.

You have nice breasts, he says.

Just then she feels a drop of rain.

Reaching for her shirt, she says, we better go in the house.

Just then, too, Philip drives up in the car.

It's raining, he tells them. We had to stop playing.

The affair lasts only the one summer. If Philip was to suspect or if he was to accuse her of it, she would deny it.

* * *

She is a liar.

The liar says: *This is a lie.*

She can never *get it.* If it is false then it must be true, yet it cannot be true because then it would be false—the paradox eludes her. The reason, perhaps, that mathematicians go mad trying to solve problems of logic.

Or are they trying to solve problems of Truth?

Another flash of lightning and she stands up too quickly. Dizzy, she waits a moment for the feeling to pass. Then groping her way in the dark, she goes to the bathroom. Once inside, she shuts the door and turns on the light.

The light is sudden and too bright. In the mirror, her face looks strange—pale and her eyes are enormous. She picks up her hairbrush and starts to brush her hair. What for? she says out loud to the face in the mirror and puts the hairbrush down.

She starts to open the medicine cabinet but changes her mind, the contents are familiar.

She looks at his toothbrush in the glass, at his toothpaste lying next to it—again, he has forgotten to put the cap back on the toothpaste tube—she looks away.

Drying her hands on a towel, she turns to open the bathroom door. Hanging on the hook are his striped pajama pants and a white cotton T-shirt. The T-shirt is so old it is transparent. The older and softer the T-shirts, the more he likes them. Next to the

T-shirt and pajama pants hangs the pretty, cambric nightgown she bought in Rome a month ago.

While Philip is attending lectures, Nina sightsees and shops. In addition to the nightgown, she buys an expensive brown leather shoulder bag with a gold clasp in a store near Piazza di Spagna—the leather, the saleswoman says to convince her, is indestructible. Feeling guilty, Nina does not show Philip the shoulder bag. Later, she tells herself, she will.

Now she never will.

In the Palazzo Doria Pamphili, Nina stands in front of *Rest on the Flight into Egypt* and stares at the red-haired angel and his outstretched black wings. Except for a swirl of white cloth, the angel, his back to the viewer, is naked; he is playing the violin for the Holy Family as they rest. Only Joseph and the donkey are listening; holding the baby Jesus in her arms, Mary is fast asleep.

Nina cannot move away from Caravaggio's angel.

Time for lunch, Philip says, impatient.

Wait, she pleads.

She tries to remember what the conference in Rome is about. Something to do with computational and scheduling problems: finding the shortest route that takes a salesman to every city exactly once, finding the most efficient way to pack a truck or pack a bin. Problems for which there are no algorithms, problems that do not interest her.

She packs the nightgown and the new shoulder bag in the bottom of her suitcase. No problem.

She will give the shoulder bag to Louise, all of a sudden, she decides.

The decision and its suddenness pleases her.

As for her pretty nightgown, it might as well be made out of burlap.

Take it off, he always says.

It has stopped raining and, again, she goes and opens the window and leans out. The trees stand as massive shapes in the garden; above them the sky is dark. She cannot see any stars.

All is quiet.

Shutting the window, she goes back and sits next to him, by the side of the bed.

How was your day? Again, she asks.

This time she will listen.

How was yours?

I began a triptych. The first panel is going to be a calm sea, the second a stormy sea, the third—she stops and shakes her head.

Has she drunk too much wine?

Holding up the bottle, she tries to read the label in the dark. An Italian wine: Flaccia—she cannot make out the rest.

His arms around her in bed, he whispers endearments in an Italian accent. He makes up names to make her laugh.

They are trying to conceive.

He touches her breasts.

Tell me again who Fibonacci was?

A thirteenth-century mathematician.

And what did he discover?

His hand is on her stomach.

A number sequence where each number is the sum of the two preceding numbers: 1, 1, 2, 3, 5, 8, 13, 21, 34, 55 . . .

He puts his hand in between her legs.

Tell me about the rabbits.

You start with two rabbits, a male and a female, born in January, and two months later, they give birth to another pair of rabbits, and two months later, that pair of rabbits gives birth to another pair, and each new pair of rabbits produces another pair who . . .

His fingers move quickly, confident.

The question is how many pairs of rabbits will there be in a year? In two years?

What if a rabbit dies? She is having trouble speaking, she is about to come.

The rabbits don't die; the rabbits are immortal.

After two years there are 46,368 pairs of rabbits, he says as, with a groan, he gets on top of her.

And in less than a year, there is Louise.

He finds Fibonacci number sequences everywhere: in flower petals, in pinecones, ferns, artichoke leaves, the spirals of shells, in the curve of waves.

In Louise's newborn face.

*   *   *

When Philip first holds her in his arms, she is a day old. He weeps.

She has never seen Philip cry before nor has she since—not when his brother Harold died, not when his father died. Then, he looked pale and perturbed but he did not shed a tear.

The last time I cried—really cried—he tells Nina, is when my dog died. I think I was fourteen. The dog was a mixed breed— half German shepherd, half something else. His name was Natty Bumppo. He was a great dog—he had a sense of humor. He used to bare his teeth and grin at me.

How about when Iris died? she wants to ask but does not.

She pictures him, dry eyed and stricken, in his one dark suit as he slowly makes his way down the church aisle.

Instead, she asks, How did the dog die?

Not too bad, Philip says, as he puts the booties on Louise's tiny feet. A perfect fit.

What are you going to knit her next? Nina asks. A sweater set?

Across from the hotel where the conference was held, Philip explains, there was a crafts shop. I have no idea why I went in—something must have caught my eye—a big basket full of wool right by the door. Big balls of natural wool and the woman in the shop said knitting was relaxing. Anyone could knit. She sold me the needles, the wool, the instructions. I went back to the airport and while I waited for my flight I began to knit and, she was right, it helped calm me down. On the plane, too, as luck would have it, the woman seated next to me offered to help. I had dropped some stitches, she said.

What, Nina wonders, caught Philip's eye? Or, more likely, who? A lonely, talkative woman who sells wool and who dresses in an earth-tone smock and wears noisy wooden clogs? To her outfit, Nina adds an abstract-shaped silver pendant—the work of an artist friend—dangling on her unsupported breasts. She is not Philip's type. Instead, Nina imagines, a tidy blonde with an engaging, bright smile, who sits next to Philip on the plane and points out the dropped stitches.

Gray, shapeless, despite the fact that Nina washes them repeatedly, the booties smell of oil and sheep. The first time Louise wears them outdoors as Nina is pushing the stroller, one of the booties slips off her foot, drops in the snow, and is lost.

Natty Bumppo was poisoned. Someone, Philip tells her, threw poisoned meat out of a car window. A lot of the dogs in the neighborhood died. So did a few cats and squirrels. The street was a mess, full of dead animals.

Did Philip know he was dying?

He looks composed, his eyes are closed. He does not look afraid. He looks the way he does when he is asleep. Perhaps he is, she thinks, and this is a mistake.

A terrible mistake.

Philip, she calls to him.

Philip.

And did his entire life flash by in front of his eyes? Or just a few memorable incidents: falling out of the tree, solving his first quadratic equation, the first time he has sex. . . .

*   *   *

Was he happy?

Did she make him happy?

They are happy on the windswept island of Pantelleria, in the two-room *dammuso* they rent for a week. The *dammuso* is built from local volcanic stone and the thick walls keep the house warm in winter and cool in summer, the vaulted roof allows the rain water to fall into a cistern below. There is no running water. Every morning, Philip hauls several buckets of water and brings them into the bathroom and into the kitchen. The bathroom is in a separate small building; a branch full of purple blossoms that grows outside serves as a curtain for the window and provides privacy.

Capers grow on the terraced hillsides; the vinelike bushes are abloom with blue flowers.

Iris.

No. She forces herself not to think of her now.

The capers are large, grainy, salty; they eat them every day for lunch with tomatoes, bread, and olive oil along with the local wine. Afterward they lie down in the dark cool thick-walled bedroom and sleep—a heavy, drugged sleep—for the rest of the hot afternoon. When they awake, they make love—slow, solicitous love—then, still naked, Philip gets up and hauls up more water from the cistern so they can both wash.

They swim in warm green inlets, aquamarine caves, and dark, colder grottoes that are divided by outcrops of rocks and lava pillars with Arab names. Above them rise the sheer cliffs of the island; perched on one is the village of Saltalavecchia—old lady's leap—where at midday they stop to buy bread and fill the car up with gas.

Perché lei é saltata in mare? Nina asks. *Un marito perso?* A lost husband? *Un figlio perso?* A lost son?

The baker shrugs his shoulders, he does not know.

Nor does the garage attendant, or he has forgotten.

Saltalavecchia is just a name, a boy, pumping air into his bicycle tires, tells her. Like Firenze or Venezia or, for that matter, Roma. He says this without looking at her.

One morning, a thin brown and white dog comes and sits on the terrace steps. Nina fetches a bowl of water for him.

Careful, Philip says. You never know here.

He looks friendly enough.

During breakfast, she feeds him some leftover toast, buttered toast.

Now, you've done it, Philip says.

What shall we call him? Nina asks.

Philip shrugs and shakes his head.

Roma, she says. It's just a name.

At night, curled up like a ball, the dog, Roma, sleeps outside their door; during the day, he stretches out flat on his side soaking up the sun on the stone terrace; from time to time, he sits up to scratch himself. He eats everything: tomatoes, bread, rice, fish—whatever Nina gives him. He eats greedily, wagging his tail. When Nina and Philip leave to go swimming or, in the evening, when they go out to dinner, he lies on the top step leading up to the terrace, his head resting on his paws, and waits for them.

What's going to happen to Roma when we leave? Nina asks. Maybe we could take him home. We could find a vet, a crate, a—

No, no. Philip shakes his head emphatically.

Although Nina makes inquiries, no one wants a dog.

Another mouth to feed! is what they all say.

At last, Anselmo, the waiter at a restaurant they frequent, agrees to take him, and on the last day, a few hours before they are due to leave, they put Roma in their car and drive to Anselmo's house. Nervous, Roma sits panting and drooling in the backseat. Half turning, Nina pats his head as he tries to lick her hand.

He knows, she tells Philip.

He'll be fine, Philip answers.

You'll have a good home, Roma, she says.

They have difficulty finding Anselmo's house, which is located in the interior of the island, a desolate, uncultivated area they have never been to before. The dirt road is rutted and bordered by stunted, twisted olive trees. It is near the airport, which, however, remains invisible to them, even as a small plane flies in low over their heads, nearly—or so it seems—grazing the roof of their car, its wheels down, ready to land.

We're going to miss our plane if we don't find his house soon, Philip says.

Anselmo, his wife, and his children are pleased to see them arrive. They offer refreshments but Philip and Nina are in too much of a hurry.

La prossima volta, Philip promises.

Anselmo and his wife laugh. The children make a show of putting their arms around Roma and hugging him.

Before leaving, Philip hands Anselmo an envelope full of money. Money to look after the dog, he says.

Non si preoccupi signore, Anselmo repeats, *il cane sará felice con noi.*

* * *

Io sono felice, tu sei felice, egli è felice, noi siamo felici, she repeats to herself. In school, she learned how to conjugate Italian verbs and recite them by heart.

And which past tense should she use now—the near past *io sono stato felice*, or the past perfect *io ero stato felice*, or the remote past perfect *io fui stato felice*?

Or, still yet, the conditional past *io sarei stato felice*.

Several weeks go by before Nina telephones the restaurant—Anselmo does not have a home phone—and she is told that Anselmo no longer works there. Anselmo, the person who answers the phone says, left a month ago. When she tries to ask about the dog, the person who answers the phone says he knows nothing about a dog.

Taking another sip of wine, Nina again thinks about how Philip, a Midwesterner, was drawn not to fields of grain or to vast green plains but to the sea and to islands: Martha's Vineyard, Belle-Île, Pantelleria.

And how he became a keen sailor.

His Hinckley Bermuda 40 has a sleek, French-blue hull, a solid butternut and teak interior, and shiny bronze fittings. The boat sleeps four comfortably, six uncomfortably, and, on it, they have sailed the cold waters of Maine and Canada—even, once, as far as Nova Scotia where, on account of the Gulf Stream, the water was surprisingly warm.

Hypatia—Philip names the boat after the first known female mathematician.

But, unfortunately, Hypatia met a gruesome end, Philip tells Nina.

How?

She was attacked by an angry mob of monks who peeled off her skin with oyster shells. She was skinned alive, then dismembered and burned.

How horrible. Why?

Her teachings were considered heretical. She wore men's clothes and drove her own chariot through the city of Alexandria. She did not know her place as a woman.

For a while, Nina resists sailing with Philip but, in the end, she gives in.

In the end, too, she grows proficient: taking the wheel while Philip puts up the sails, catching the mooring without his having to come about twice, reading charts and cooking meals on the tricky gas stove. She walks *Hypatia*'s deck on her sea legs without holding on to the wire guardrail, and, finally, she has grown accustomed to falling asleep to the lap-lap of the waves against the boat's hull and has grown to like the sound.

Hypatia, Nina mouths to herself.

Bradycardia, she says.

Once a month, on Sundays, Philip stays in bed for most of the day—Winston Churchill, he has heard, did the same. Not to have sex, but to restore himself.

Philip has breakfast and lunch in bed, but by midafternoon the bed is full of crumbs, spilled drinks, the Sunday paper, books, journals, pencils, his laptop, and Philip is forced to get up. While he showers, Nina tidies and makes up the bed.

I feel like your maid, each time she tells Philip, who has come out of the shower and is drying himself with a towel—a towel he drops on the floor.

He is whistling a tune.

You should have married Paul Erdös, Philip teases her.

Paul Erdös, he tells her, lived out of a suitcase. Instead of a shirt, he wore his pajama top; he had no money, did not eat meat, washed his hands compulsively, and did not know how to tie his own shoelaces. But he wrote or coauthored 1,475 academic papers. More than any other single mathematician in history.

Philip has published with someone who has published with someone who published with Paul Erdös.

Philip's Erdös number is 3.

Lorna, too, lived out of a suitcase—or nearly. Disorganized, unreliable, brilliant, she worked at the Center for Particle Astrophysics in Berkeley until she overdosed. The housekeeper found her in her bed; Lorna had been dead for several days already. Hard not to picture the decomposing body: Lorna's curls framing her once beautiful, now discolored and disfigured face.

Accident or a suicide? Everyone who knew Lorna was curious to know.

So is Nina.

Why do so many mathematicians commit suicide? Is it because their discoveries make them feel isolated and alienated? Or is there some other reason? she asks Philip.

Instead of answering, Philip says, I should have gone over to her apartment when she did not answer the phone. I had a feeling something was wrong.

Philip spends that night in his office working—or so he says. Or, perhaps, he spends the night driving around Marin, where Lorna lived. In the morning, when he finally comes home —Nina hears him climbing up the stairs to the bedroom—his limp more pronounced than usual.

Suppose we were to fly through the entire universe in a spaceship, Lorna says one evening, early on in the semester, when she comes to Nina and Philip's house for dinner, the way the early explorers circumnavigated the globe, we might just end up where we started. She laughs nervously, waiting for Philip to reply.

Are you saying that the universe is finite, edgeless, and connected? Philip asks her.

Earlier, Nina notices that Lorna's shoes, ballet flats, are of two different colors—one black, one silver.

She hesitates before pointing this out.

Oh. Looking down, Lorna's face turns pink. I must have been thinking of something else.

What else did Philip and Lorna talk about? Theories of the early universe, chaos, black holes.

Nina has set the table; she has cooked the dinner—a picky eater, Lorna does not eat meat or fish. After they finish the main course, Nina gets up and clears the dishes.

But isn't it absurd to think that the universe might be infinite, Lorna says, returning to the same subject as she pokes at the dessert on her plate with her fork.

A pineapple upside-down cake Nina has baked especially.

For if, say, we go beyond Einstein's theory—if we find an ultimate theory of everything—the theory will prove that we humans are created from the same basic substance as the universe, and that we and the universe are just different manifestations of the same thing. How then could the universe be infinite when we ourselves are finite?

Lorna speaks in short, almost inaudible, nervous bursts, so that one has to lean in close to hear what she is saying. She is small-boned and her arms are covered with freckles. She does not know how to drive a car and after dinner, Philip takes her home. To Nina, it seems as if the drive takes him longer than necessary. He is gone for two hours.

The traffic, he claims when he finally comes home. And an accident on the highway.

You shouldn't have mentioned her shoes, Philip also tells Nina. You embarrassed her and it was childish.

But, by then, Nina has decided that Lorna is the child. A careless, needy child who cannot exist in the actual world or with the people in it.

You don't understand, Philip says, frowning when, later, she again brings up the dinner with Lorna. Physicists do not have the freedom mathematicians have. Physicists deal with the actual world while mathematicians choose their worlds.

* * *

Downstairs, she hears a noise. The house settling or a piece of old furniture? The tall mahogany highboy in the dining room, she guesses. One of the drawers is filled with the Russian niello silver spoons that Philip collects.

Collected.

The spoons are carved with intricate patterns of flowers and leaves; some are even more intricate, with castles, hunting scenes, and—Philip's favorite—a full-rigged sailing frigate. On special occasions—Christmas, New Year's, a dinner party—Philip carefully places the spoons on top of the pristine white linen napkins Nina uses to set the table.

For decoration only, he warns the guests. Niello is made from one part silver, two parts copper, and three parts lead. Should you use the spoon to eat your soup you will risk brain damage.

Everyone but Nina laughs.

In spite of herself, she glances at the clock. The luminous dial points to a few minutes past two.

She does not feel tired.

On his mother's side, Philip's grandfather was a well-known silversmith. The Revolution in 1917 put an abrupt stop to his work and he left Russia for America. He managed to take some silver with him—spoons, a snuff box, various items he had worked on. When his children got married, he gave them each a piece of silver. His mother, Philip says, got a spoon.

What happened to it? Nina asks.

She may have lost it. Or she sold it.

Next time we visit, you should ask her.

Philip shrugs. She may not remember.

Nina will ask Alice.

Better yet, she decides, she will bring Alice one of Philip's spoons.

Look, Alice, she will say, Philip found your old silver spoon. The one with the full-rigged sailing frigate carved on the back of the bowl.

Nina's parents died several years ago. She rarely thinks of them—not, she tells herself, because she did not love them. She did. Retired, they lived in Florida. Her father played a lot of golf; her mother played board games and bridge. They were self-sufficient and uncomplaining. Eventually, they moved to a retirement home where Nina, once or twice a year, dutifully visited them. On the last visit—by then, her father had died of complications from a stroke—she walked on the beach and played Scrabble with her mother. Despite a recent hip replacement, which caused her to tire more easily, her mother won the game handily with the seven-letter triple-word-score *xerosis*. Challenging her, Nina lost. Xerosis means abnormal dryness of the skin—a condition her mother suffered from.

Downstairs, the noise again. Nina tenses. The front door is not locked. Anyone, she thinks, can walk in. How ironic—if that is the right word?—were a thief or, worse, a murderer to break in.

Would he assume that Philip is asleep and shoot him? Kill him twice. As for her, the murderer would first demand money, jewelry, before tying her up and shooting her as well. In the head, quickly, she hopes.

She does not want to think of the alternative.

In town a few years ago, in the spring, a young vagrant knocked on an elderly woman's door asking for yard work. After pruning her lilac bushes and trimming her hedge, he put the same sharp clippers to her throat and raped and sodomized her. Soon after, the elderly woman died. She never recovered from her torn cervix and rectum or from her shame.

She listens for another sound, a door shutting, footsteps on the stairs, but hears nothing. Getting up and putting her hand against the wall for balance, she walks to the hall and looks over the banister. From where she stands, she can see the front door and, next to it, the large Italian ceramic pot that serves as an umbrella stand.

The pot is from a shop in Pantelleria. Nina has kept the owner's card. Piero? Pietro? she no longer remembers which. She remembers that he flirted with her a bit.

Ah, *signora,* he says, holding her hand up to his lips, welcome to my shop.

Are you English? he also asks.

No, Americans, Philip tells him.

Americans. I have shipped to Ohio, to Nuova York, to California. Ah, beautiful California.

Have you been? Nina asks, freeing her hand at last.

Piero or Pietro shakes his head. No, no. My brother, he live in California.

Despite her look of disapproval, Philip does not bargain and pays for the pot in cash.

You'll see, he is never going to send it to us, Nina tells him as they get back in the car. I don't trust him.

You never know, Philip, an optimist, answers.

Months later, the pot arrives, intact. It is packed with newspaper and straw in a large handmade wooden crate.

You have to have more faith in people, Philip tells Nina.

Iris again.

What if she finds a photo of Iris? The photo slips out from in between papers, from inside a folder in a desk drawer. Or what if Louise, who is helping her sort through Philip's papers, finds it—a small, 2½-by-2¼ black-and-white photograph.

Look, Mom. Who is this blonde girl standing next to Dad? She looks like Grace Kelly. I love her dress. So fifties. Look at her tiny waist. Dad's got his arm around her. Is she a relative? There's something written on the back. It's hard to make out— "To my darling." Yes. "To my darling Phil."

Yes, a relative, Nina tells Louise.

And, no, not Grace Kelly, Nina thinks. Grace Kelly is too sophisticated and well heeled. Iris looks more like Eva Marie Saint—the way Eva Marie Saint looks in the movie *On the Waterfront*: pretty, naïve, and full of convictions.

Eva Marie: the name of Philip's best man's fourteen-year-old daughter who was killed in an avalanche as she skied down the unpatrolled backside of a mountain in Idaho. Getting buried in snow, Nina thinks, must be like drowning.

* * *

When Philip is away and she is alone in the house at night, she moves the umbrella stand directly in front of the front door. If an intruder was to come in, he would knock over the umbrella stand and break it. The noise will wake her.

Undecided for a moment, Nina stands in the hall and looks around. The door to Louise's bedroom, the doors to the guest room and guest bathroom are all shut.

Three doors.

She shakes her head a little, recollecting.

How many times have I tried to explain this to you?

She can hear the bantering and slightly irritated note in Philip's voice.

You have three doors in the game and behind one door is a car, a diamond ring, or—

How about a new washing machine? Nina interrupts.

Okay, then, there is a new washing machine behind one door and a goat behind each of the two other doors.

One of those expensive German ones. A Bosch.

Are you listening or not? Otherwise, I am not going to try to explain this to you again.

I am listening.

Okay, so you choose a door. The door stays closed but since the game show host knows what is behind each door, he opens one of the two remaining doors—one with a goat behind it. He then asks you if you want to stay with the door you chose or if you want to switch to the last remaining door.

I would stay with the door I chose, Nina says.

Don't you see, Nina, Philip goes on, raising his voice, once the game show host has opened one of the doors that has one of the goats behind it, he has reduced your chances from 1 in 3 to 2 in 3 to open the door with the washing machine? It's to your advantage to switch. It's obvious. I can explain it to you logically. I can explain it to you mathematically.

Still, Nina refuses. I told you, I am not switching doors.

What does he call the problem? A veridical paradox, for although it appears to be absurd it is demonstrably true. And what does he call her?

A stubborn goatherd.

Back in the bedroom, Nina pulls up one of the chairs and places it next to the bed.

Again, she touches Philip's cold hand.

Philip, she whispers.

He wants to be cremated, he has said so. He also says that he does not want his ashes to be buried but spread in the sea. In the Atlantic, he specifies.

The largest park in Paris. It's over a hundred acres, Philip informs her, as they stroll through the Père Lachaise cemetery on a sunny spring day soon after they meet.

A veritable history lesson among the seventy thousand graves, he says.

They have taken the métro and walked down the boulevard de Ménilmontant; outside the entrance a woman is selling flowers. Philip stops and buys Nina a bunch of red carnations.

Hand in hand, they walk up and down the avenues of tombs, reading off the names out loud to each other: Marcel Proust, Édith Piaf, Honoré de Balzac, Oscar Wilde . . .

In front of the elaborately carved mausoleum that houses the remains of Abélard and Héloïse, they pause for a moment. The tomb is surrounded by an iron fence but is littered with flowers and bits of paper that have been thrown inside.

I read in the guidebook that those pieces of papers are letters to Abélard and Héloïse written by people who want their own love to be requited, Nina tells Philip.

And I read that those are not Abélard and Héloïse's remains, Philip answers.

Cynic.

And with one sure, swift gesture, Nina tosses the carnations inside the mausoleum. The flowers clear the iron fence and land squarely on top of the carved prone figures of the lovers.

Good throw, Philip says. Then, taking her in his arms, he adds, Your love is requited. Is mine?

I'm hungry, he also says before she can answer. Let's go and have lunch.

Over the years, they have visited the cemetery several times. Each time, they walk down different avenues, look at different tombs: Colette, Richard Wright, Simone Signoret, Félix Nadar, Max Ernst . . .

The walks in the cemetery inspire them—perversely

perhaps, in the face of so much death—with a kind of childish hilarity. They tell jokes, play games: Which is the most ornate tomb? the most tasteless? their favorite?

Philip's favorite is the highly polished, black marble tomb shaped like a triangle, of Sādeq Hedāyat, a Persian writer who committed suicide.

Nina's favorite is the tomb of the Armenian general Antranik Ozanian.

He looks like Vittorio De Sica. The mustache.

I thought you didn't like mustaches, Philip says.

I like the statue of the horse, she says.

Instead of following the others, Philip's horse puts his head down and resolutely begins to eat the grass. Philip is afraid of horses. And horses sense his fear and take advantage of him.

Pull his head up! Give him a kick! The cowboy leading their group on a trail ride yells at Philip.

Nina has persuaded Philip to spend the week of Louise's spring break at a dude ranch in Arizona.

Louise wants to go. And it's a change, she says.

Nina is riding a lively pinto named Apple. Right away, the cowboy notices her seat, her hands.

I see you've ridden before, he says.

Louise, also, rides well.

Philip's horse, a big sorrel gelding, refuses to move and the cowboy trots over on his own horse and, determined, he cracks his whip over the sorrel's hindquarters. Jerking his head up in surprise, the sorrel bolts forward and Philip loses his balance. To keep from falling off, he grabs at the pommel.

Dad! Louise says, before she starts to laugh.

Turning her head away so that Philip cannot see her, Nina, too, laughs.

Keep him moving, the cowboy tells Philip. Shorten your reins, keep his head up.

Show him who's boss, Phil, the cowboy adds.

Few people call Philip Phil.

Did Iris? *My darling Phil.*

Mon petit Philippe—Nina thinks of Tante Thea. Generous and kind, she takes Nina and Philip to the theater, to the ballet, to expensive restaurants. She takes Nina shopping. When Tante Thea dies, she leaves Nina her diamond pin in the shape of a flower.

When did she last wear the pin? Nina tries to recollect. To a black-tie dinner honoring one of Philip's colleagues, a Nobel laureate in physics.

Tell me again what he won it for, Nina asks as she tries to open the safe.

For the discovery of asymptotic freedom in the theory of the strong interaction.

For what? Say that again. And is it three turns to the left to 17? Or three turns to the right to 17? Nina says.

Asymptotic freedom shows that the attraction between quarks grows weaker as the quarks move closer to each other and, conversely, that the attraction grows stronger as the quarks move farther apart. Are you ready, Nina?

Nearly.

The discovery established quantum chromodynamics as the correct theory of the strong nuclear force, one of the four fundamental forces in Nature.

Didn't he and his wife write a book together? Philip, I still can't get this safe open.

Yes—about how scientists arrive at their theories of the universe and why there is something instead of nothing. His wife, too, is a brilliant mathematician. Nina! What are you doing in there? We are going to be late, Philip almost shouts.

Here, let me.

How many times have I showed you? Philip says more quietly, when he has the safe open. It's so easy.

Easy for you, Nina says, suddenly close to tears.

I just don't want us to be late, Philip says.

In the car on the way to the dinner, fingering the diamond flower pin to make sure it is securely fastened to her dress, Nina says, Let me tell you about my theory of the universe, Philip.

Her theory of the universe is that there is no theory.

Their last visit to Père Lachaise is on a winter day. The tree limbs are bare; the cypresses loom dark and forbidding. The pots of too-bright artificial flowers placed around the tombs make the sky, by contrast, appear grayer, more somber.

Damp and cold, Nina shivers in her down coat. Don't you want to be buried next to me? she asks.

They are stopped in front of the tomb of Gertrude Stein and Alice B. Toklas.

Putting his arm around her shoulder, Philip says, And don't forget to throw my ashes to leeward or else they'll blow back in your face.

Sitting next to the bed, she shuts her eyes for a moment and replays the scene of their meeting in Paris.

Vous permettez?

Je vous en prie.

Ordinary and familiar phrases that give her pleasure.

What is your book about? he also asks her.

Afterward, they walk together along the boulevard Saint-Germain toward the boulevard Saint-Michel. She notices his limp but says nothing. By then, they have established that they are both familiar with the same city back home, the same shops and restaurants, which may be enough reason for them to see each other again. On the way, they stop at a bookstore where she locates the works of Nathalie Sarraute. She pulls *Tropismes*, the book she is reading, off the shelf for him.

I'll buy it, Philip says. A promise to her, perhaps, that they will see each other again.

She should reread *Tropismes*, she thinks, opening her eyes.

She should make a list: *War and Peace, Anna Karenina, Middlemarch;* all of Dickens, Jane Austen, Trollope . . .

The novels of Balzac, Zola, Flaubert.

* * *

A few days later, they argue.

Did you read it? Nina asks Philip.

They are having dinner together in an inexpensive restaurant in the Latin Quarter, a few blocks from the gallery where she works. It is late and she is tired.

Read what? Philip is looking through the wine list. Is a Côtes du Rhône all right?

The book you bought. *Tropismes.*

Already, she has decided that she is not going to sleep with Philip. She orders the snails cooked in garlic.

Philip frowns and shakes his head. I tried, he says.

He orders the soup.

I couldn't get past the first page.

Really? You couldn't read it? Nina is offended. Those beautiful interior monologues?

They're incoherent, Philip answers.

Ils semblaient sourdre de partout, éclos dans la tiédeur un peu moite de l'air—he recites.

And who is this cousin of yours related to her by marriage? She interrupts, changing her tactic. I am not sure I believe you.

I'll introduce you, he says, smiling.

Many years later, in Boston, Nina goes to hear Nathalie Sarraute read. Old, elegant, and imperious is how she describes her to Philip.

I am not surprised, he says.

Oh, and what about her cousin? You never did introduce me to him, remember? Or did you make him up?

She not he, Philip says. The cousin is a *cousine.*

* * *

Tante Thea's eighteenth-century yellow stucco country house stands at the end of a long driveway bordered by chestnut trees; her property abuts the forest of Chantilly. Lunch on Sundays tends to be a long and lively affair, with plenty of food, red wine, and, for dessert, a homemade fruit tart topped with heavy cream. Family, friends, neighbors sit crowded together around the mahogany dining room table, everyone talking fast and at once about de Gaulle, *the nouveau franc*—worth 100 of the old franc and how confusing Tante Thea finds it still—the Algerian crisis and how garbage cans have been placed on the runways at Orly Airport to keep the Algerian rebel paratroopers from landing—and to keep everyone else from landing, one of Tante Thea's sons points out.

Didier and Arnaud, Tante Thea's sons, are there for lunch. Both are married, successful, and athletic. Didier especially. He and Nina flirt a little and Anne, his wife, does not seem to mind.

Didier is in love with Nina, she teases.

In spite of herself, Nina is attracted to Didier's self-assurance, his sturdy good looks, and the way he wears his tailored blue shirt, the sleeves rolled up to reveal his forearms.

After lunch, complaining of tennis elbow, Didier persuades Philip to be Anne's partner in a game of doubles against Arnaud and his wife; upstairs, Tante Thea is taking a nap, and he asks Nina to take a walk in the forest with him—only he doesn't ask her.

We'll go for a walk, he says. A little exercise will do me good, he adds.

It is late in the spring but some of the chestnut trees are still in bloom and their blossoms mingle with the leaves of the trees to form a canopy over the forest floor, a green carpet densely packed with low bushes, grasses, and clusters of delicate little white flowers that Nina does not know the name of.

Neither does Didier.

Crisscrossing the forest are well-maintained paths—*allées* they are called—some of the names are marked on signposts.

It must be easy to get lost, Nina says.

I've walked here ever since I was a child, he answers. I know the forest by heart. In the fall, I go hunting here.

Fox hunting?

Stag hunting.

They talk about the different American schools. One of Didier's daughters wants to go to college in the States. Nina describes the one she went to.

Then, coming toward them, they hear the sound of galloping hooves.

Careful, Didier says, taking Nina's arm and drawing her to the side of the path as two riders, crouched jockey style, gallop past them.

The sandy soil is good terrain for training horses, Didier says, still holding on to Nina's arm.

She starts to answer how she, too, likes to ride, but Didier has pulled her to him and is kissing her. She tries to pull back but he has hold of her arm and is twisting it behind her, forcing her to lift her face up to him. His mouth presses so hard against hers that she feels his teeth. Then, half dragging her farther into the forest, he forces her to the ground.

Nina hits the side of her head on something.

Didier! she cries out. Don't, please!

I wanted to make love to you from the first moment I saw you, he says.

Already, he is on top of her and, with one practiced hand, he pushes up her skirt and is pulling down her underwear.

At first, she struggles against him; then, looking past him at the treetops overhead, she lets him.

Afterward, walking back down the *allée*, Didier stops to pick a few of the delicate white flowers that neither of them knows the name of and he puts some in Nina's hair.

Kissing her lightly on the cheek, he says, Now that wasn't so bad, was it?

Shaking the flowers out of her hair, Nina does not answer him.

In the rented car on their way back to Paris, Philip asks, How was your walk with Didier?

Fine.

They are stalled in traffic, long lines of cars ahead and behind them. A few motorcycles weave noisily and triumphantly in between the cars; drivers honk their horns uselessly. Also, it has begun to rain, a light drizzle.

How is it everyone always drives home from the weekend at the same time? Philip asks. I should make a study of the probability. He turns on the windshield wipers; they make a grating sound on the glass.

Perhaps there's been an accident. I hate that noise, Nina says.

Glancing over at her, Philip asks, What did you two talk about?

Me and Didier? He asked me about American colleges for Cécile, his daughter. Next year, after she passes her Bac.

The cars begin slowly to move again.

Doesn't that jerk know how to signal? Philip makes an angry gesture with his hand at the driver in front of him.

We saw some horses galloping down the *allée*—they were racehorses, I think, Nina volunteers.

Those *allées* were designed by André Le Nôtre for the Prince de Condé, Louis XIV's cousin.

I know, you've told me.

Is something wrong? Philip says.

A headache, Nina answers, touching the side of her head. I think I'm getting a migraine.

Sometimes, when Philip comes back from being away, she sniffs through his laundry, searching for the scent of an unfamiliar perfume—patchouli, jasmine, tuberoses.

What is her name?

The name of a city.

Sofia.

Lies of awful omission.

She had an abortion.

She pours the last of the wine.

Should she tell him?

In the dark room, she tries to make out Philip's features.

Can he hear her?

* * *

Somewhere—where she cannot recall—she has read how each of us is a bundle of fragments of other people's souls, the souls of all the people we have known.

She does not believe this.

She is not a fragment of Didier's soul.

Didier died a few years ago, of colon cancer, and Nina wrote Anne, his wife, saying she remembered how he was full of joie de vivre and how he always embraced life.

Embraced *her*, she thinks.

Outside, she hears a car slowly drive by. Nina goes to the window and, parting the curtains, she catches a glimpse of the taillights before they disappear into the dark. Who, she wonders, is out at this time of night? And where are they going? There are only a few houses on the road and, at this hour, she supposes, all their occupants are asleep.

The first city that was home to her was Atlanta; next came Cincinnati; then her family was sent abroad. First, they went to Montevideo, later they moved to Rome, still later to Brussels. Nina's father worked for a multinational company that manufactures household products: soaps, cleaning powders, detergents. As a result of all the moves, Nina learned to speak Spanish, Italian, and French but because she had to change schools so often, she never learned to speak any of those languages properly. Also, it was difficult for her to make friends; she spent her time reading, daydreaming.

What has made her think of this?

The car's disappearing taillights?

Early on, when she was eight years old and living in Uruguay and long before she had heard of solipsism, she devised the idea that only she existed in the world. A war, an appalling crime, or, merely, a dish falling and breaking on the ground, a door slamming in the next house, occurred for her benefit alone. Everything else was a void, a huge emptiness, nothing.

She remembers little about Uruguay: the balcony overlooking the street outside the dining room and how once she threw a glass of water on a boy walking below—angry, the boy had looked up and shouted, *Puta, puta;* her school pinafore with her name plainly embroidered in thick red thread on her chest—*Niña, niña,* she was teased; the maid picking her up from school and teaching her how to roll her Rs.

RRRR—she curls her tongue and rolls the Rs out loud.

She has not forgotten how and this pleases her a little.

CaRRRavaggio—she tries again.

A little impatient, Philip claims that the painting is too sentimental. He much prefers, he says, the vigorous realism of *The Conversion of St. Paul on the Way to Damascus* and *The Crucifixion of St. Peter*, the two Caravaggio paintings in Santa Maria del Popolo.

I can't explain it, Nina says as they leave the gallery, but there is something about the angel that is very sensual. Erotic almost, she says. He is so robust—the way he stands, nearly naked, on one leg, his hip jutting out. But his black wings look too small, too delicate, as if they were painted on as an after-thought . . . Nina does not finish.

On the way to the restaurant—or perhaps the theft takes place while they are in the Palazzo Doria Pamphili—Philip is pickpocketed, his wallet stolen. Only after they have eaten and it is time to pay does he notice that the wallet is gone. He then has to spend the better part of the afternoon at the police station; he has to cancel his credit cards—already someone has charged thousands of euros worth of appliances—and he misses several important lectures.

I should have paid more attention, he tells Nina, patting his jacket pocket.

Diane, the other woman who works with Nina in the art gallery, goes with her. Her boyfriend, a medical student, has given Diane a phone number. When Nina dials it, a man answers. After asking her how many weeks she is pregnant, he gives her an address and tells her to come at two o'clock the day after next, which is a Wednesday—*mercredi*. In addition, he tells her to buy disinfectant and cotton—there is a pharmacy on the corner of the street—and to bring two thousand new francs in cash. He never tells her his name.

He might have killed her.

Fortunate, except for fog, they rarely encounter bad weather. Once, only, are they caught in a storm—the tail end of a Florida hurricane—with waves crashing on the deck, the wind tearing at the sails, the boat heeling so far over it takes on water.

Poor *Hypatia,* Philip says. She came close to being skinned alive a second time.

In the dark, she shudders and drinks a little more wine.

The boom breaks Philip's nose and his front tooth; down below, Nina is thrown against the edge of the stove top and cracks a rib.

The hospital in the Maine coastal town is small, the staff efficient and friendly. Nothing can be done about her cracked rib except warn her not to cough or laugh. She is given pain pills. Philip's nose is set by inserting a metal rod up his nostril; she hears him cry out. He is lying next to her in the emergency room. As for his tooth, the dentist at home will fashion an expensive cap for it.

Leaning over the bed, Nina touches Philip's face; with her finger she traces the outline of his nose. No one could guess that he broke it.

Over and over, she tries to do Philip's portrait in oil; each time, dissatisfied, she puts the painting aside. The quick sketches in charcoal are better. The problem is Philip's mouth—she can never get it right—his lips curl in an unnatural way. The last time she paints him, she wants to do him nude.

Take off your shirt, your pants, she tells him, your shoes and socks.

Your boxer shorts, too, she adds.

Standing with his hands on his hips, Philip refuses to take them off.

Don't be silly, Nina says.

I don't feel comfortable standing here naked, he complains. And it's cold.

Nude not naked, Nina replies. And think of me as a professional and not as your wife.

How can I think of you as not my wife? Philip asks.

I don't know. Aren't you supposed to have an imagination?

Still, he refuses to take his boxers off.

Recently, at an exhibition, Nina saw a painting Lucian Freud did of his mother after she had died. A beautiful and serene portrait of a wrinkled, old woman with her eyes closed, her hands crossed over her chest, lying on her back on a narrow iron bed.

She cannot imagine painting Philip now.

The boxer shorts Philip wears while he poses for her are light blue but she paints them bright red—a carmine red—the closest she comes to have him nude.

Lorna again.

She runs into them unexpectedly in a popular health food restaurant. Sitting across from each other in a booth, they are eating lunch—not touching. What distresses her is how animated they look. When they catch sight of her, abruptly, they stop talking.

Philip waves her over.

What are you eating? Nina cannot think of what to say.

Garbanzo bean stew—do you want to taste it? Philip holds a spoonful out to her.

No, thanks. Nina makes a face.

* * *

Philip's metabolism is good; he does not gain weight. He eats what he wants and eats everything.

She remembers the chicken getting cold downstairs—the sauce and fat congealing together on the platter. She prefers the white meat, the breast; Philip prefers the thigh and drumstick.

How well suited they are.

Louise, she thinks.

Oblivious, Louise is asleep, content after sex, in the arms of a handsome young man. In the morning, everything will change. The handsome young man will be forgotten as Louise quickly packs her suitcase, drives to the airport, and flies back home.

Louise, Philip's darling. Always strong and sensible.

When she was two years old, Louise came down with spinal meningitis. Nina did not recognize the symptoms right away—fever and vomiting. At the time, she thought Louise had a stomach flu or had eaten something that did not agree with her.

Then Louise had a seizure. Then she went into a coma.

For once, Nina prayed. In the hospital chapel, on her knees, she prayed and prayed. She lit candles for Louise. She made God all kinds of promises she could not keep.

God in heaven, Nina says to herself.

God in heaven, she repeats, not sure what she means.

* * *

Green pastures filled with contented white sheep is how she sees it. Wearing dresses, the color of candy, Iris and Lorna are waiting for Philip.

Like in a bad novel.

But going through the motions—attending church, kneeling, praying—is what, according to Philip, Pascal recommends for people like her who still question the existence of God.

She tries to remember the words of the psalm: *The Lord is my shepherd; I shall not want. He maketh me lie down in green pastures*—she shuts her eyes to think but she has forgotten what comes next.

A different song begins to sound in her head:

> *Won't you lay your head upon your savior's breast*
> *I love you but Jesus loves you the best*
> *And we bid you good night, good night, good night. . . .*

Hadn't they once gone to a Grateful Dead concert?

A hot and humid summer night, the air thick with the smell of pot. The Hearst Greek amphitheater is packed with people waving their arms and screaming. Nina can hardly hear the music, much less the words—only she knows most of them by heart. She keeps her eyes fixed on one of the musicians, the piano player. His hair is long and parted in the middle; he looks stoned.

She pictures herself in bed with him.

And we bid you good night, good night, good night, she and Philip sing in the car on the way home.

They come close then to getting separated.

Her only friend in Berkeley is the mother of one of Louise's classmates. Dark-haired and thin, Patsy is divorced. She lives in an apartment complex a few blocks from Nina and Philip's house; she has a younger boyfriend, Todd. Todd works at Mammoth as a ski patrolman; on his day off, he comes and stays with Patsy. He always arrives with marijuana and other forbidden substances in his worn black backpack.

Where does he get all that? Nina has to ask.

From skiers who break their legs and give him their stash, Patsy tells Nina. They don't want to go to the hospital with that stuff in their pockets—the nurses will confiscate it or, worse, report them to the police.

Nina's drug of choice is amyl nitrite, which comes in the form of a little blue capsule that she breaks in half and sniffs up her nose. Right away she gets a rush. Her blood vessels expand, her heart beats faster.

Poppers are good for sex, Patsy also tells Nina. They relax the sphincter muscles.

The what . . . Nina starts to ask.

While their daughters are in school, they also smoke marijuana.

Pot makes Nina laugh.

Stretched out on Patsy's living room floor, on the yellow synthetic rug that has a sour chemical smell, the window shades drawn, the room dark as night, she listens to a recording of wolf howls. The howls—a whole series of them—are described by a narrator with a clipped British voice.

A howl of alarm, he says.

Never, never—*ha ha*—has she heard anything so funny.

A chorus of howls.

Ha ha ha—she laughs.

Hoo hoo hoo—she howls like the wolves.

Next to her on the floor, Patsy and Todd are making out. This, too, makes her laugh.

She never speaks of it to Philip.

She never speaks of it to Dr. Mayer.

Too late, come to think of it now, amyl nitrite is used to treat heart disease.

Again, she tries to remember exactly what he says when he comes home.

I am a bit tired, I am going to lie down for a few minutes before dinner, or does he say something else entirely?

She is spinning lettuce in the kitchen. She half listens.

What a day. All those meetings! You should hear how some of those physicists talk and talk.

Before going upstairs, he kisses her on the cheek.

She touches her cheek. This cheek.

Philip! Dinner! she calls to him.

Philip, darling! Dinner!

* * *

Darling, dear, sweetheart, honey—endearments she rarely uses.

Nor does Philip.

Ma chérie, he says.

Ma chérie is how he addresses her in the letters he writes when he returns to the States in the summer. He writes her two or three times a week—telephone calls are expensive and, anyway, she does not own a phone. She cannot always read the letters that are written in black ink on both sides of onionskin paper in his small cramped handwriting; the blue airmail envelopes are addressed to *Mlle. Nina Hoffman, 8 rue Sophie-Germain, Paris 14ème, France.*

He looks pleased when she tells him where she lives. A sign, he says.

A sign of what? Nina asks.

You don't know whom the street is named for?

Nina frowns. No. She does not.

Sophie Germain was a famous eighteenth-century mathematician who set out to prove Fermat's last theorem by saying that *n* is equal to a particular prime number and since prime numbers have no divisors. . . .

Nina lives in a *chambre de bonne* six flights up narrow airless dark stairs; she has to share the toilet and the tub with the other occupants on her floor.

A sign of my not having a whole lot of money, she interrupts Philip.

* * *

"One of the most important correspondences in the history of mathematics," Philip tells his students, "was between Blaise Pascal and Pierre de Fermat. It began on August 24, 1654, and its object was to find a solution for the problem of the unfinished game.

"Take two players and place equal bets on who will win the best-out-of-five coin tosses. The players start the game but are forced to stop before either player has won, leaving one of them ahead 2 to 1. The question Pascal and Fermat pose is how will the two players divide the pot?"

Patsy never has enough money and Nina lends her some. And for a while, after she and Philip leave Berkeley, Nina stays in touch. Then Patsy moves to Santa Fe, then to Phoenix; Nina's last letter is returned with *Address Unknown* stamped on the envelope.

"The way Pascal and Fermat solved the problem was to look at all the possible ways the game might have turned out had the two players finished and tossed five times. And since one player—let's call her Louise after my six year old daughter—is ahead 2 to 1 after the three tosses—tosses that must have yielded two heads and one tail—the remaining two throws can yield—"

H H   H T   T H   T T—Philip writes it out on the blackboard.

"And since each of these four tosses is equally likely, we can proceed thus: in the first, H H, Louise wins; in the second and third, H T and T H, Louise still wins; in the fourth T T, the other player wins. This means that in three of the four possible ways the tosses could have come up Louise wins, and in only one of the possible tosses does the other player win. Louise then has a 3 to 1 advantage and the pot should be divided 3 to 4 to her and 1 to 4 to the other player. Are you following me?"

Silence.

"The point I want to make to you," Philip says after a pause, "is that Pascal and Fermat's letters first showed us how to predict the future by calculating the numerical likelihood of an event occurring and, more important, how to manage risk."

In her *chambre de bonne*, the narrow bed covered in an Indian fabric is pressed up against one wall and doubles as a couch; across from the bed, there is a scarred wooden bureau; on top of that, an electric hot plate, a few dishes, two china cups, and a radio. A wooden armchair stands by the window and stacks of books are piled on the floor; on the shelf over the sink are her toiletries, soap, a packet of brown toilet paper, a few bottles of water, a bottle of Johnnie Walker Red, a half-empty jar of Nescafé, and a hand mirror. Several posters from the art gallery where she works, advertising upcoming shows, are thumbtacked to the wall. From the hooks nailed to the door dangle some hangers with skirts, dresses, her leather jacket; also, a man's hat.

Picking up the hat, Philip asks, Who does this belong to?

From her window, she looks out on to mansard roofs and, craning her neck, she can also look down at a private interior garden that, except for a small white dog who occasionally runs mania-cally around it, is always deserted. In the building directly across from her she can see into a dining room where, in the evening, a family—mother, father, and three children—eat their dinner. She watches as they talk, laugh, pass their plates, and refill their glasses.

In the morning, often late, she takes the métro to work, then, afterward, if it is not raining or cold, she walks home. That spring, she takes to wearing a man's hat—it makes her, she thinks, look modish.

Except for those he wrote her long ago, she has received few letters from Philip. From time to time, a postcard from some far-flung place where he is attending a conference, which she does not al-ways keep. One of these postcards—a postcard with a picture of a junk sailboat on it—arrived long after Philip himself gets home.

> Last night I had dinner on the Peak in the house of a
> wealthy Chinese lawyer who is a trustee at the university
> here and his Eurasian wife. They have a fabulous collec-
> tion of jade; also of Ming china. We ate off some of it.
> Dinner consisted of all kinds of exotic dishes including
> rooster testicles! The weather is glorious. I suggest we
> move to Hong Kong immediately. All my love to you and
> Lulu, Philip

Sofia, again.

A slender, dark-haired woman, in a tight-fitting silk *qipao*, eating rooster testicles with her slippery ivory chopsticks.

What do they taste like?

The rooster testicles? I don't know. Rubber bands.

Does she speak English? Nina also asks.

Of course. She studied at Oxford and speaks several languages—English, French, Spanish, I think she said. To say nothing of Cantonese and Mandarin.

And the Ming china. What does it look like? Nina presses.

Blue and white. Philip frowns slightly, then says, which reminds me of how, once, according to Sofia, a guest at one of their dinner parties picked up a Ming bowl to look underneath for the mark and he dropped it. The bowl broke and, according to Chinese custom—so that the guest does not feel embarrassed and to show that he is not overly attached to his possessions—the host is supposed to break his own bowl.

And did she?

Philip shrugs. Yes, I suppose.

The poor guest. He must have felt terrible.

And what would you do under those circumstances? she asks.

I would go to an antique store and try to replace the Ming bowls.

Like turning the other cheek.

Would she have? No, probably not. She is too easily angered, too quick to take offense. A true redhead, her parents were always quick to remind her.

The result of a genetic mutation since neither one of them had red hair.

* * *

Redheads make up 5 percent of the world population, Philip tells her, as they lie pressed together on her narrow bed in the maid's room on rue Sophie-Germain. Scotland, he also says, twisting a strand of her hair between his fingers, has the highest population of redheads. A redhead in Corsica is considered bad luck but redheads are good luck in Poland.

I should move to Poland.

Redheads are more likely to be stung by bees, Philip continues. And the Egyptians burned all redheaded women.

I won't go there, Nina says.

No matter now, her hair has turned gray.

"My wife has red hair—auburn is what she prefers to call it," is how Philip begins another lecture. "As you can see, I have black hair although it is starting to turn gray"—the students laugh. "Our daughter, Louise, who is twelve"—here Philip pauses a moment—"no, she's thirteen now, also has black hair, which leads me to today's subject—the role played by probability in heredity. You all know how Gregor Mendel, the nineteenth-century abbot from Moravia, began his experiments with two peas: a yellow pea and a green pea and how he cross-fertilized these two peas and got all yellow peas, then how he cross-fertilized the second-generation peas and got three-quarter yellow peas and one-quarter green peas. This was not a new experiment but so far no one had explained it, until Mendel did. He showed how the seed of an offspring of the two original peas—the yellow and the green—contain the following combinations: yellow-yellow, yellow-green, green-yellow, green-green; and that the seed which contains a yellow gene will almost always produce a yellow pea because yellow is the dominant color. . . ."

Before she gets into bed, Nina turns up the volume of a popular music station on the radio to drown out the noise of their lovemaking.

Taking off his shoes and socks, his shirt then his pants, Philip sings along with Johnny Hallyday singing "Let's Twist Again."

He makes her laugh.

Mimicking the way Johnny Hallyday pronounces *year* to sound like *yar*, Philip climbs into bed next to Nina.

In the room next door, the Swiss au pair pounds on the wall.

She's just jealous, Philip says as, undeterred, he gets on top of Nina and slowly begins to move, making the narrow bed bang against the wall.

Nina starts to laugh again.

Stop, Philip tells her, as he holds her tighter and moves faster inside her, making the bed rock and sway and bang harder against the wall.

Or I'll come.

Yar, he says.

Again the Swiss au pair pounds on the wall.

The shutter again.

Who said sounds are magnified at night?

Philip?

No, Andrew.

A dog has begun to bark. The neighbor's old yellow Lab, she guesses.

She cannot think of his name.

Poor poisoned Natty Bumppo.

She cannot leave the bed, she cannot reach the sink, she throws up in the wastepaper basket by the side of the bed. Next, she throws up in the bed. All day and all night, she retches painfully, violently, until there is nothing left inside her but bile and she feels as if she is retching up her insides. She is certain that she is going to die.

At last, she falls asleep; then she hears knocking.

God, Philip says. What happened?

What time is it? Outside, it has begun to get dark, it must be the next day.

I called the gallery and they said you hadn't come in yesterday or today.

I was sick, she says. A migraine.

She feels weak but better. The room is airless and smells of vomit. Slowly, carefully, she swings her legs out of bed—legs that look to be too thin to support her weight—and goes to open the window.

Let me take a bath, then I'll clean up this mess, she says.

I'll give you a hand, Philip says.

* * *

He runs the bath for her and holds her steady as she steps into the warm water.

Lie back, lean your head on my arm, he says.

You'll get wet.

Rolling up his shirt sleeves, Philip kneels at the side of the tub and washes the vomit stuck to her hair.

Shut your eyes, relax, he tells her.

Have you thought of becoming a nurse? Nina asks.

Did you see an aura? Philip asks. Like with epilepsy, you are supposed to see one.

Nina, her eyes shut, is only half listening.

A few lights, maybe, she answers.

Epileptics were considered sacred. Some people think they still are. In Laos, for instance, the Hmong, Philip continues.

Lying in the tub filled with warm water in the cramped bathroom on the sixth floor of the apartment building on rue Sophie-Germain, her head resting on Philip's arm, Nina comes close to telling him what happened to her in the forest of Chantilly but she does not.

Instead she says, How do you know this?

I knew a girl who had epilepsy.

Opening her eyes, Nina asks, Who?

A girl called Michelle in my English class, Philip answers. She was acting out the sleepwalking scene about washing the blood from Lady Macbeth's hands when, all of a sudden, her eyes rolled back inside her head and she fell, her body jerking on the floor, and for a moment, we all thought it was part of the act, Michelle playing Lady Macbeth, but, of course, it wasn't.

When I was in high school in Brussels, I played Lady Macbeth, Nina says, standing up.

Voici l'odeur du sang encore, tous les parfums de l'Arabie ne sera pas adoucir cette petite main, she recites, giving Philip her hand to hold as she gets out of the tub. Funny how I remember those lines.

Your hand smells sweet only it's wet, Philip says, leaning over and kissing it.

For a long time after, Nina is convinced that the migraine headaches are a punishment for her lies.

The neighbor's dog is still barking—the sound is closer. They must have let him out of the house; otherwise, he will wake up their baby.

She thinks of the dog in Pantelleria—lying in a ditch, she supposes, run over.

Migraine is what she calls the series of large red near-monochrome canvases in which she combines layering, smearing, and drip painting. The paintings take up most of the wall space in her studio and are unlike anything else she has done.

An experiment, she tells Philip, when she shows them to him.

Interesting but disturbing, he says.

She takes this to mean he does not like them.

* * *

She never has a migraine while she is pregnant with Louise.

Again, she takes this for a sign.

After Louise is born, however, the migraines come back, worse.

Now she has medication.

Alerted, this afternoon, by the familiar flicker of lights and a slight throbbing in her head, she leaves her studio and gives herself an injection, then she lies down on the sofa in the living room. The sofa is worn, the pattern, an old-fashioned chintz, is faded. She plans to get it recovered but, as yet, has not done so. A part of her does not want to make changes and Philip does not appear to notice or to mind how shabby some of their furniture—furniture they have had since they were first married—looks. The living room curtains, too, she reflects, just before she falls asleep, need to be replaced. The sun has rotted their linings.

When she wakes up, the headache is gone and, relieved, she remains on the sofa a while longer to enjoy the feeling of well-being. Piled up on the coffee table, next to her, are a stack of science journals; picking one up, she leafs through it. She skims an article describing how experiments surgically joining together old and young mice are used for regenerative biology research, then, turning the page, some photographs of Japanese crop art catch her eye. Each year, she reads, the farmers in the small village of Inakadate, Minamitsugaru District,

Aomori Prefecture, located at the northern end of Honshu, plant purple-and-yellow-leafed kodaimi rice with green-leafed tsugaru-roman rice to create huge images based on works by famous Japanese artists. The images, according to the article, are first plotted on computers then marked with reed sticks on the rice paddies.

Did you see this? she plans to ask Philip when he comes home. *You could try it with lettuce: red leaf, romaine, Bibb. . . .* Instead he goes upstairs to lie down.

Philip prides himself on his garden. On warm spring weekends, he is out early, tilling, hoeing, planting, weeding. In the summer, they have more vegetables than they can eat.

The photograph she wants to show Philip is of a Sengoku-period warrior on his horse. The horse is made from the yellow-leafed kodaimi rice and is portrayed with mane and tail flying, his purple-leafed kodaimi rice nostrils flared.

Now who will tend to the vegetable garden?

She makes herself think of something else.

French gardens.

Parc Montsouris, with over a hundred different varieties of trees and shrubs from all over the world—except for the weeping beeches, she cannot recall any of them—is Philip's favorite.

Her favorite is the Jardin du Luxembourg.

Closing her eyes, she retraces her steps.

* * *

In the spring, while it is still light and the gates to the park are not yet shut, she walks from the rue Jacques-Callot where she works and makes a quick left turn onto busy rue de Seine, then hurries to cross boulevard Saint-Germain and continues until she reaches a narrow shop on the corner of rue Saint-Sulpice that sells antique jewelry, and where she pauses a moment to admire the art deco bracelets, rings, and, in particular, a brooch in the shape of a dragonfly with emerald and ruby wings— wishing she could have it—until one day, it is gone from the window and she mourns it—mourns its loss as if the brooch had been hers. Once she catches a glimpse of a slender young blonde woman—no older than she—sitting by the window inside the shop, her head bent, stringing pearls. Reminded of someone—only she can't think who—and attracted by how swiftly the woman moves her hands, again, she stops and, no doubt sensing Nina's presence, the young woman looks up and smiles at her through the glass. A few more steps and rue de Seine turns into rue de Tournon, a wide elegant street that is flanked by old houses and expensive shops. At the next corner, a café. Then, straight ahead, the imposing Senate building, and, to one side, the entrance to the Luxembourg. At this time of year, the pear trees are in bloom and brilliant red and yellow tulips line the paths. When she comes to the boat basin, she pulls up two of the green metal chairs—one to sit, the other to put her feet on—and watches the children, who are still out prodding their boats in the brackish-looking water with long, wooden poles, and she can hear the mothers scold. Always, a man drags over a chair to come and sit next to her.

Vous avez l'heure, Mademoiselle?

She feigns incomprehension.

Voulez-vous prendre un café?

Often, the man follows her part of the way through the garden and Nina pretends not to notice.

A silly joke comes to her unbidden: an American girl, warned of the dangers posed by French men, learns a word to say in French to discourage their advances. The word is *cochon!*—pig!— and, sure enough, when a man on the métro gooses the girl, she turns to him and shouts, *Couchons!*

Although she always looks, Nina never again sees the pretty young blonde woman, sitting by the shop window, stringing pearls.

Come to think of it now, the pretty young blonde woman stringing pearls reminds her of Iris.

Under the branches of the weeping beeches in Parc Montsouris, she and Philip sit, hidden, on a blanket on which they have spread out their picnic lunch. As soon as they have finished, they lie down and Philip begins to kiss her. Kisses that taste of the red wine he has drunk. Long, drawn-out kisses—his tongue pushing and probing into her mouth until she has to catch her breath.

Wait, I have to breathe, she says, pushing him away.

Reaching for the bottle, Philip drinks more wine.

Nodding absently to herself, Nina takes another sip of wine. Holding up the glass, she can see that it is almost empty.

She sighs.

Hidden as they are by the pendulous beech branches, no one can see her raised skirt, his unzipped pants. She can hear a couple sitting on a nearby bench arguing, a child riding by on his bicycle, a baby stroller being pushed past. Philip presses his head against hers, his lips in the crook of her neck and in her hair, to try to muffle the sound he makes. Looking up, she hears a bird chirp his alarm.

She remembers the cat.

Noiselessly, a skinny, one-eyed, white cat—wrinkled pink skin covers the other eye—emerges from the beech branches as they are eating their picnic. Nina throws him bits of her ham sandwich.

He'll never leave, Philip says. You shouldn't do that.

Poor thing, he looks hungry, Nina says. I wish we had some milk.

He looks sick, Philip says. I wouldn't touch him.

Instead, Nina gets to her feet and, hand extended, walks toward the cat.

Here, kitty, here, kitty, kitty.

The cat turns and runs.

Later, as Nina is shaking out the blanket and Philip is picking up the food wrappers and the empty bottle of wine, the cat reappears.

His tail up in the air, the cat walks over to Nina and presses himself against her legs.

Reaching down, she strokes him. What happened to your eye? she asks. I should take you home, she also says.

Something else about a cat.

Something she can never quite grasp.

Tell me again, she whispers to Philip.

This time, I promise, I'll try to understand.

The experiment is meant to illustrate the futility of using quantum mechanics to try to consider everyday objects. By putting a live cat in a locked box—

A live cat? How cruel.

No, I told you it's a thought experiment—by putting an imaginary cat in a box along with an imaginary small amount of radioactive material, small enough so that over the course of several hours one of the atoms in this material might or might not decay and kick off a particle, which in turn would trigger a hammer that would smash a vial of hydrogen cyanide, which would then fill the box with cyanide gas and kill the cat—

But I don't see how the—

Nina, let me finish, Philip says a little sharply.

Schrödinger tried to show that the fate of the cat depends on a microscopic event that, in turn, is dependent on the unpredictable behavior of particles. Particles aren't governed by laws we recognize, they are governed by probabilities. You can't pin them down, you can only say that they might be in this state or that state. Each of these states is assigned something called a probability wave function and understanding probability wave functions is crucial to understanding quantum mechanics. Do you understand what I am saying so far?

Well, no. I don't understand what you mean by probability wave function.

You are not alone. No one really understands it.

Are you serious?

Probability wave function cannot be understood in the normal sense because it does not make sense logically. It only makes sense mathematically.

But to go back to the cat, Philip continues. When the box is closed we do not know if the atom has decayed or not, which means that it can be in both the decayed state and the nondecayed state at the same time. And since the decay of particles is not predictable, both realities—that of the dead cat and the alive cat—can exist simultaneously. Only by opening the box can the nature of the cat's actual state be observed.

I still don't get it, Nina says, shaking her head. Or is it like the riddle of the tree falling in the forest with no one there to hear it?

That's only part of it. The tree falling in the forest may be pointing to questions of the perceivable universe but whether someone is there to hear it or not does not imply that the tree is both standing and fallen. You see the difference, don't you?

She does not like his tone. The way he emphasizes certain words to make his point and the way he speaks to her as if she were a child.

She does not reply.

Don't worry about it, Philip continues. Just think of the cat as a metaphor for the paradox inherent in quantum physics.

In her mind's eye, the cat in the locked box and the skinny, one-eyed white cat she saw one spring afternoon in Parc Montsouris are one and the same.

It must be very late.

She is tempted to cry out.

But once she starts, she is afraid she will not stop.

They would be in bed by now, asleep.

As soon as Philip gets into bed, he falls asleep. Sometimes he snores a little.

Nina wakes up during the night. She always wakes up on the half hour: at three thirty, four thirty, five thirty.

She often gets out of bed, slowly removing the covers so as not to disturb Philip, and, in the dark, gropes her way downstairs. In the kitchen, she opens the refrigerator and finds something to drink, then crossing the front hall to the living room, she turns on the light and lies down on the sofa to read.

She reads whatever is at hand. Books, magazines, recipes: *daube de boeuf à la provençale* cooked with garlic and anchovies makes her mouth water.

Daube, she repeats to herself.

She plans to make it one day.

A surprise for him.

Besides the rooster testicles, what else did you eat? Nina asks.

Bird's nest soup. Delicious, Philip says, smacking his lips. The nests are made out of saliva—birds' saliva.

Nina makes a face.

They're supposed to contain high levels of calcium, iron, and magnesium, and to have certain medicinal properties, Philip says, paying her no attention, like aiding digestion, alleviating asthma—

She pictures Philip scraping the last of the edible swiflet's nest from the bottom of a precious blue-and-white Ming bowl.

—and raising the libido.

According to Sofia—the woman whose house we had dinner in—the mark at the base of a piece of Chinese porcelain, Philip continues, changing the subject, designates the reign of the emperor at the time the piece was made. After dinner, she took me around the house and showed me some of the more valuable—

What was the house like? Nina interrupts.

Very modern, all glass, elegant—but let me finish. The bowl I particularly remember came from the Chenghua period—that's the fifteenth century—and it was so fine you could see through it, but the mark at its base was very rough and the reason for this, Sofia explained, was that it was made by the emperor when he was very young and his handwriting had not yet developed properly.

Philip has finished his bird's nest soup and again she pictures how he picks up the bowl and holds it up in the air to look underneath at the mark.

Philip drops the bowl and the bowl breaks.

"Imagine a teacup falling on the floor and smashing into random pieces," Philip tells his class. "If you were to film this, you could run the film backward and see all the pieces jump back together. Obviously, you cannot do this in ordinary life—believe me, I've tried although my wife complains that, soon, we won't have any china left." No one laughs. "The explanation for this," he continues, "is that disorder or entropy within a closed system always increases with time—in other words, left alone, everything will decay. The teacup, which looks like such a delicate object is, in fact, a highly ordered thing. It took energy to make it that way and when the teacup breaks, some of that energy is lost and the teacup is in a disordered state. The increase of disorder or entropy with time is an example of what is called the arrow of time. The arrow of time distinguishes the past from the future and . . ."

Time, Nina says as she pours Philip a cup of coffee in the morning, is what prevents everything from happening at once.

Philip looks up from his newspaper. Where did you hear that?

I didn't hear it. I read it.

Where?

Graffiti. In a public toilet.

You're joking.

"However, should the universe stop expanding and start to con-tract," Philip continues, "disorder or entropy would decrease and, then, like in the film played backward that I mentioned earlier, we would see broken teacups everywhere coming back together. We would also be able to remember events in the future but not remember events in the past."

For the weekend, she has rented Bernardo Bertolucci's *The Con-formist* and *Blue* by the Polish director whose name she cannot pronounce and which begins with *K*.

Krzysztof Kieslowski—both his names.

Philip, she guesses, will choose *The Conformist*. He likes Dominique Sanda. He saw her in *The Garden of the Finzi-Continis*—and what did he say about her?—she is cool and sexy.

On the whole, Philip prefers blonde women.

She would choose to see *Blue* again, her favorite among the three films that make up the trilogy: *Red, White,* and *Blue*.

In her mind, a large French flag flaps noisily in a sudden gust of wind—*liberté, égalité, fraternité*.

Blue stands for liberty and, in the movie, Juliette Binoche plays the part of a woman who has lost her husband and daughter in a car accident.

* * *

Louise is alive.

But what if the plane she takes tomorrow crashes? A malfunction on takeoff or wind shear on landing? What if, on the way to the airport, she has an accident? Distracted, Louise does not see the stop sign at the intersection or, not her fault, a driver, driving drunk, crosses the double line and smashes into Louise's little red Jetta? What if—

She must stop herself from thinking things like this.

In the dark, she tries to see Philip's face.

Again, she is reminded of Schrödinger's experiment.

If Philip were to remain unobserved, like the cat in the locked box—although she knows that the radioactive substance that may or may not set off the vial of hydrogen cyanide is an essential part of the experiment—he would be both dead and alive at the same time.

How can that be?

But our brains—how often has Philip tried to explain this?—cannot function in the world of quantum uncertainty. Quantum mechanics is a mathematical construct that embraces two incompatible alternatives, assigning to each its probability.

Only if we accept an interpretation of quantum mechanics, he goes on to say—but she has stopped listening and is thinking about something else: how to mix her paints to get the right carmine red? how long to keep the *daube de boeuf* in the oven?—can we begin to imagine that an infinite number of variant replicas of ourselves are living out their parallel lives and that at each moment more of them leap into existence to take up their optional futures.

Aliens. Science fiction.

In an alternative universe, in another reality, Philip is shorter, younger, blond. He is a plumber, a real estate agent, an airline pilot. He is married to someone else.

And he is alive.

And yet?

Holding her breath, she strains to see if there is any movement under the diamond-patterned quilt.

If Philip is breathing.

Juliette Binoche looks good in a bathing suit. In the movie, she swims in a public pool as a way of trying to assuage her grief. The water and everything around her is blue.

A peaceable color blue.

What, she tries to think, is the word for the blending of two senses?

Philip would know.

Richard Feynman, one of Philip's teachers, saw equations in color—light tan js, violet bluish us and dark brown xs flying around. In addition to attending his seminars at Cal Tech, Philip often goes to Richard Feynman's house to hear him play the bongo drums.

Synesthesia, she remembers the word all of a sudden.

* * *

Iris, never mind the individual letters, is, of course, blue. A light, celestial blue, the same color as the Virgin Mary's blue cloak.

The blue of the Caribbean is different—it is a greenish blue, an aquamarine blue. A glittering blue.

The blue of Jean-Marc's eyes.

They have vacationed on various islands: St. Martin, Guadeloupe, Martinique—French islands.

Islands again.

Sunbathing on Marigot Beach, Philip, unashamedly, stares at the topless French women.

You're staring, Nina tells him.

Lying next to him on her stomach, she is reading *Speak, Memory.* Nabokov also attributed numbers and letters with special colors—*s* and *c* are shades of blue, *f, p,* and *t* are green, *e* and *i* are yellow, *b* and *m* are different shades of red. From time to time, she glances over at Philip.

Did you forget your book?

No. Shaking his head, Philip holds up his paperback, *The Moving Toyshop.* On vacation, he reads mysteries.

She hears Philip turn pages but when she looks over at him, she sees that he is no longer reading. He is staring out again. Following his gaze, she, too, watches a slender young woman who is standing knee-deep in the water. The young woman bends over and splashes water on herself, on her small brown breasts, before she steps farther out into the sea. She is wearing a bikini bottom with a red flower motif on it that only covers part of her buttocks. Shouting out, a darkly tanned, robust young man runs past her, splashing, and, grabbing her arm, he drags her with him into deeper water. When they resurface, they are laughing.

Nina looks away.

They will be kissing next.

Turning over, Nina lies on her back and, emboldened by the French women, she takes off the top of her bathing suit. Her breasts look shockingly white in contrast to the rest of her body, which is tan, but they are firm enough.

Nina! Philip exclaims, when he turns to ask her to pass him the suntan lotion.

What?

You can't go topless.

Why not? Everyone else is.

Yes—but it's not decent to have everyone looking at your breasts.

You look at everyone's breasts—what's the difference?

That's not the point.

What is?

You know perfectly well what I mean.

Getting up, Philip walks off.

I broke my leg falling out of a tree, he tells her. I was horsing around with Harold and I landed wrong.

Did he push you?

We had sticks. We were jousting with each other.

Up in a tree?

We were always doing crazy stuff like that.

Didn't you get along with Harold?

Yes, I got along with him. We just fought all the time, the way brothers do.

Poor Harold. She does not want to think of him lying in the grass outside the wedding tent, drunk, with his fly open.

Irish twins—Philip and Harold were born fourteen months apart.

She has seen a black-and-white photo of them as young boys—Philip looks to be about twelve and Harold must be eleven—dressed in overalls, their arms around each other. Behind them is a house with a large front porch and, on it, an old-fashioned metal canopy swing. Philip is a head taller than Harold and he is holding Natty Bumppo, who sits between them, by the collar. Both boys are squinting into the sun.

The photo was taken on my grandparents' farm in Wisconsin, Philip tells Nina. We went there every summer.

At about the same age, while she is living in Montevideo, Nina makes up a twin for herself. The twin is identical, her name is Linda.

Linda, in Spanish, is beautiful—*muy linda*.

Linda is good company and Nina confides in her. She is Nina's closest friend and the only other person who exists in the world.

They are inseparable.

Linda, she whispers.

Linda, she says a little bit louder.

There is no answer.

Tilting her head back, Nina drinks the last of the wine.

The bottle is empty.

At the time, she blames Linda for throwing the glass of water from the balcony at the boy below in the street.

Linda also shoplifts an expensive black-and-gold pen for which Nina is punished.

Feeling hot, she goes to the window and opens it, letting in a cool breeze that causes the curtains to again billow out. She stands there for a moment wrapped in their folds. Everything is dark and quiet and feels unreal.

Then—after closing the window and the curtains—a little unsteadily and holding on to the bedposts, she makes her way around to her side of the bed. Kicking off her shoes, she eases herself onto the mattress and lies down next to Philip.

Again, she reaches over and touches his cheek.

Cold.

His hands.

Very cold.

She sighs deeply and closes her eyes for a moment.

Sex.

She does not want to think about sex.

Yet she does.

They are in bed naked.

Where?—Paris? Pantelleria? Belle-Île?

Pantelleria.

Hot, very hot. It is four o'clock in the afternoon according to the alarm clock on the table by the bed and Philip reaches over and touches her stomach. A little pool of sweat lies in the hollow between her hip bones.

God, it's hot, he says.

Opening her eyes slowly—she feels drugged by the sun, the wine at lunch—she focuses on the beaded curtain at the entrance of their room, which gives directly onto the terrace. The room is full of moving shadows, bits of light pierce through the beads making jittery patterns on the walls, the floor, the bed. Outside, it is still too bright. Something red is lying on a chair on the terrace—her discarded sarong. She hears the dog shift his position as he lies by the doorway, guarding it. She smells the sea, the earth, and rot.

Philip turns to her. His face open, calm, expressionless, like one of those Flemish portraits of a medieval saint. He puts his arm around her and starts to kiss her—her mouth, her breasts, her navel, and, farther down, her cunt. He does not shave every day and his face is rough against her skin but she doesn't mind. She holds his head tight between her legs as she comes. When he gets on top of her, she takes his penis in her hand.

Don't. Let me, he says.

Inside her, he starts slowly, looking down at her face as if he is examining it for the first time and she looks back up at him. They don't speak as, covered in sweat, their bodies smack against each other faster and faster until he comes. Afterward, he lies on top of her, motionless, like a dead person, his head resting heavily on her shoulder and she does not move.

When finally he rolls off her, he says, I'm happy.

She replays the scene once again in her mind.

And again.

She makes a few changes.

She is on top of him, rising up and down on her hands and knees, her breasts swinging near his face; she is lying on her stomach, her face pressed into a pillow, as he enters her from behind.

But always there is the same suffocating heat; always the same shattered light in the room separated from the terrace by the beaded curtain; always the dog nervously shifting his weight outside; always a glimpse of her red sarong draped over the chair and the acrid smell of sea, earth, and rot.

After, he tells her, I'm happy.

For once, he is not thinking about numbers; he is not counting.

* * *

And always, carefully, she sniffs the air.

Blue plastic bags filled with garbage, thrown out of car windows by picnickers, dot the single main road of Pantelleria. Long before they are collected, the bags burst open in the sun or a dog or a wild animal chews through the thin plastic to get at what is inside. If the wind is right, she can smell the rotting garbage all the way to the house.

In a ditch, the carcass of the dog, Roma.

The room has begun to spin and she opens her eyes.

Sitting up, she places the pillow squarely behind her back.

She drinks too much at an annual faculty lunch party to which spouses are invited.

A party to celebrate *pi* on March 14 at 1:59 p.m. exactly.

A silly tradition, she tells Philip.

And the date of Albert Einstein's birthday, he answers. A nice coincidence.

My turtle Pancho will, my love, pick up new mover, ginger, a young assistant professor recites. The nonsense phrase is a mnemonic based on a phonetic code for the first 27 digits of the mathematical symbol *pi*.

My movie monkey plays in a favorite bucket, a pretty young PhD candidate laughingly takes up another mnemonic for the next 17 digits.

Que j'aime à faire apprendre un nombre utile aux sages!
Immortel Archimède, artiste ingénieur,

Qui de ton jugement peut priser la valeur?
Pour moi, ton problème eut de pareils avantages

The head of the department, a man Philip dislikes, declaims in perfect French.

Excusing herself, Nina gets up from the luncheon table to go to the bathroom as Philip taps his glass with his fork and prepares to stand.

He has agreed to recite the first one hundred digits of *pi* by heart.

31415926535897 . . .

She is splashing cold water on her face from the sink when the young assistant professor comes in.

I think you've made a mistake, he says, smiling. This is the men's room.

Looking around, she notices the urinals for the first time; she also notices the graffiti on the door to one of the stalls.

So it is, she answers, blushing. Sorry.

. . . 640628620899.

In the dining room, people are clapping. Philip must be finished.

A hundred is nothing, Philip is saying as Nina sits down at the table. So far Hideaki Tomoyori of Japan holds the record. He has memorized the first forty thousand digits of *pi*.

It takes him nine hours to recite them, Philip adds, laughing. And during all that time, he never takes a break to eat, drink, or take a leak.

Time is what prevents everything from happening at once—she wants to remember what was written on one of the stall doors in the men's room.

* * *

The phonetic code, Philip maintains, is useful as it turns meaningless numbers into meaningful words and can be used to
remember phone numbers, postal codes. For example, he tells
Nina, 1 is *t* or *d*; 2 is *n*; 3 is *m*; 4 is *r*; 5 is *l*; so that it follows that
my is 3 and *turtle* is 1, 4, 1, and 5, and so forth. Every digit is as-
sociated with a consonant sound and that is how I can remember
the first hundred digits of *pi*.

By the way, where did you go? Philip also asks.

The bathroom. I got my period, she lies.

This is a lie, the liar says.

Nina had her own code for remembering numbers—only she
does not try to explain it to Philip.

The first 8 digits of *pi* would go like this: she is pregnant at 31; now, she is 41; 59 are the last two digits of Patsy's
telephone number; and 26—she has to think for a minute—2
plus 6 adds up to 8, and 8 is the street number of the building on rue Sophie-Germain where she used to live. Or, she
can subtract 2 from 6 and get 4 and 4 is the floor she has to
climb to on foot—the elevator is out of order according to a
handwritten sign taped to the door—to reach the apartment
in the building around the corner from the pharmacy where
she buys cotton and disinfectant. And since the number of that
building is 58 she can invert the 2 and the 6 and subtract the 4
and this will be another way to remember the next few digits
of *pi*. And didn't she have to take the number 6 métro from
Denfert-Rochereau to La Motte-Picquet to get to 58 avenue
Émile Zola? And, as for the 2—come to think of it—didn't

Émile Zola have 2 illegitimate children, a boy and a girl, with his wife's seamstress, his mistress?

For Nina, this is more than enough to remember.

She remembers the difficulty she has when she leaves the apartment, going down the four flights of stairs. On each landing, she sits down on a step and waits for a few minutes. The bleeding has not stopped.

The names of Émile Zola's children are Denise and Jacques.

She and Philip wanted two children.

A brother or a sister for Louise.

"Suppose that, after many years, I meet an old friend," is how Philip begins another class, "and the friend says to me: 'I hear you have two children and the oldest is a girl' and I answer, 'Right, my oldest daughter is named Louise.' Now the question is what is the probability of my second child being a girl? The answer is easy. The probability is 1 to 2. But, say, I vary the question a little and my old friend does not know whether Louise is the eldest or not and he simply asks: 'I hear one of your children is a girl,' the probability of both children being girls becomes 1 to 3."

Holding a bucket in one hand, Louise steps cautiously into the sea. She is three or four years old and she is naked.

Where are they? Belle-Île?

A wave comes in and swirls around her sturdy little legs and, dropping her bucket, Louise retreats hastily to the beach.

Lying on their towels, a few feet away, Nina and Philip are watching her.

Getting up, Philip runs down to the edge of the water and retrieves the bucket for Louise, who has turned to them, her mouth set to cry.

Quickly, Philip picks Louise up in his arms and walks into the sea with her.

From where she is sitting, Nina waves at them but they are not looking back at her.

Standing waist deep in the sea, the waves breaking against him, Philip lifts Louise up in the air, out of the water's reach, and he sings to her

> *Pi pi find the value of pi*
> *Twice eleven over seven is a mighty fine try*
> *A good old fraction you may hope to supply*
> *But the decimal never dies*
> *The decimal never dies*

as, shrieking from both fear and delight, Louise clings to him, her chubby arms locked around his neck.

Thank God for Louise.

Watching them, Nina is jealous of her daughter.

"Conditional probability is attached to a person's knowledge of an event and is revised according to new pertinent

information that will affect the said event, so if my old friend
were to ask me: 'I hear one of your children is a girl born on
a Wednesday. . . .'"

Taking off her underwear and lifting up her skirt, she lies down
on a rubber sheet that is cold and clammy against her buttocks
and that is spread over what looks—although she is too afraid
to look—to be a flimsy folding cot.

The man wears a dark vest over his shirt. He wears rubber gloves—the kind to do dishes with. A woman is with him.
She wears a yellow cardigan sweater and she nods absently
at Nina.

The man and the woman speak to each other in a foreign
language.

Arabic, Nina thinks.

She closes her eyes.

Probably the man and the woman are Algerian, she decides.
Pieds-noirs.

Barefoot, Sephardic Jews are said to have fled Spain to settle
in Algeria and Nina tries to picture them as they walk, from one
continent to the other, over water.

She hears the clinking of instruments in a metal
basin.

The man says something to her as, with his hands, he forcibly spreads her legs wider apart.

She keeps her eyes shut.

The woman in the yellow sweater, she guesses, is handing
him the instruments.

* * *

OAS—Organisation de l'Armée Secrète—she has heard Didier and Arnaud, his brother, speak of the right-wing underground group during Sunday lunch at Tante Thea's.

I am not in favor of Algerian independence, declares Didier as he carves the *gigot,* but I am also not in favor of the methods of the OAS. Their use of torture.

The FLN is no better, Arnaud says. Front de Libération Nationale, he explains for Tante Thea, his mother.

I know, Tante Thea answers tartly. I read the papers.

Someone in my office received a pipe bomb at his home. Fortunately, it did not go off. His wife and children could have been killed. Make mine *bleu,* Arnaud also tells Didier about the meat.

One of my students, a *pied-noir,* at the École Polytechnique, Philip says, told me that they are throwing Algerians into the Seine with their hands tied behind their backs so they will drown.

Nina is passing around the plates with the slices of *gigot* on it. Looking down at the near-raw meat on the plate she is holding, she feels sick.

I saw you crossing the Yard, Farid, Philip's student from the École Polytechnique, tells him. At first, I didn't believe that it could be you until I looked in the telephone book and here you are, Farid says, pleased to have rediscovered Philip.

Philip has invited Farid to their Somerville apartment for dinner.

At the door, he takes off his shoes.

No need, Nina says.

Farid is not wearing socks. *Pieds nus.*

Your parents—are they both French? she asks as they go into the dining room.

My father is French, my mother is Algerian—Arab.

It was terrible how they had to live then—there were curfews and the police always stopped them for their papers, Farid shakes his head. I had to leave.

She is exhausted—the baby does not sleep through the night—but she has pressed and put on a clean white shirt, a pair of black pants that still fit. She has made lamb stew, rice, baked eggplant.

So, tell me, what are you doing now? Philip asks Farid as soon as they sit down at the table to eat.

I'm working for a professor at Dartmouth who rarely bathes or shaves and whose beard reaches his waist—Farid and Philip both laugh—on how to assign probabilities to sequences of symbols that describe real world events that can be mapped to predict what comes next given what one already knows.

Algorithmic probability, Philip says, nodding and helping himself to food. To solve artificial intelligence problems.

In the next room, Louise starts to cry.

Excusing herself, Nina leaves the table to go and nurse her.

When she returns, Philip and Farid have finished dinner and are in the living room drinking the Algerian wine Farid has brought as a gift.

Nina clears the table and washes the dishes before going back in the living room. Busy talking, neither Philip nor Farid look up.

Since according to Kolmogorov's concept, the complexity of any computable object is the length of the shortest program that computes—Philip is saying.

I just want to say good night, Nina interrupts.

She could have worn a burqa.

Each Christmas, they get a card from Farid. Married with three grown sons and a grandchild—a photo of a dark-haired baby in the arms of a yellow-haired daughter-in-law was included in the most recent card—he lives and teaches in Montreal.

The baby's name is Chelsea.

The baby has to be Didier's—sex with Didier was unprotected.

Too soon to determine the gender—for the first trimester, the fetus has identical genitalia. The only way to tell now is to do a chromosomal analysis.

Nor did she ever think to ask.

A boy, she guesses.

Saltalavecchia, she thinks.

The old woman who leaps off the cliff—only she is young and beautiful and has no choice. She is pregnant. She has been sleeping with a married man or a man already betrothed to someone else. They meet each other on moonless nights and make love on the terraced hillside among the caper vines—he makes her a crown out of the blue flowers and places it on her head, and, although dry and faded now, she keeps the crown under her pillow. Or she is the one married. Her husband is older, impotent, he cannot give her children. Every day on her way to market she passes by one of those idle, near-handsome young men who owns a motorcycle and loiters outside the village café. One day, he calls out to her and, without thinking, she drops her shopping basket and gets on the back of his motorcycle. She pulls down her skirt to try to cover her thighs then puts her arms around him as he starts up the motorcycle and guns it down the winding island road.

Nina is afraid of heights. Not because of vertigo but because she feels irresistibly drawn to them. The truth is she is tempted to jump from windows and balconies, from high places. She wants to know how it feels to free fall through space—her body twisting, turning, somersaulting, effortlessly, like a high diver, in the air. Almost, she envies those suicides but not their terrible, bone-crushing, crashing death.

She is reminded of a poem—a poem about a stewardess who is sucked out of an airplane when the emergency door suddenly opens. The poem is based on an actual incident and it describes how, high up in the air over the Kansas cornfields, the stewardess starts to take off her clothes—a kind of death-defying striptease—first her jacket with its insignia of silver wings, her blouse, her skirt, her girdle (stewardesses were required to wear them then), and how, next, she kicks off her shoes, peels off her stockings and, finally, her brassiere, until she is naked.

Instead of a sacrificial victim falling to her death, the stewardess is both a bird and a goddess marveling at the exhilaration of flying and at her newfound erotic freedom. She is "the greatest thing that ever came to Kansas"—a line Nina remembers.

Saltalavecchia, Nina repeats.

Jean-Marc owns a motorcycle—a Moto Guzzi, an Italian make.

Walking along the harbor one evening, Philip and Nina run into him as he is parking it in the street. He is waiting for his wife who is arriving on the ferry, Jean-Marc tells them. She has been visiting relatives in Brest.

I've never seen a Moto Guzzi up close before, Philip says as he walks around Jean-Marc's motorcycle, inspecting it. I thought BMWs made the best bikes.

Let's have a drink while you wait, Philip also says.

BMWs may be the best, Jean-Marc answers, but, from my father, I have inherited an aversion to all German-made goods.

Why is that? Philip asks, although he probably knows the answer. What will you have? he also asks as they sit down at an outdoor café and he raises his arm to get the waiter's attention.

My father was interned in a German POW camp, Jean-Marc says. Bad Orb, near Frankfurt. When he returned, after almost five years, he refused to have anything to do with anything German. He would not ride in a Mercedes car.

At home, we have a Volkswagen, Nina says, but as soon as the words are out of her mouth, she regrets them. Jean-Marc, however, does not seem to hear her.

Do you want to see what I bought today? she asks, to change the subject. Out of her shopping bag, she pulls out a pair of red espadrilles. Do you like them?

That makes how many pairs? Philip says, smiling.

An infinite number, Nina replies. She, too, is smiling.

Here comes the ferry, Jean-Marc says, pointing with his chin. Here comes my wife.

Later, to Philip, Nina says, I don't see how riding a Moto Guzzi is any different. The Italians and Germans were allies during the war.

The Germans were evil; the Italians were stupid, is what Philip answers her.

Briefly, in her head, she revisits the German military cemetery with its rows and rows of black Maltese crosses that mark the stones with the names of the nearly twenty thousand dead.

Names like Dieter, Friedrich, Hans, Felix.

Happy Felix—except Felix is dead.

Looking over at Philip, she tries to imagine what it is like to be dead. Is it how it was before he was born, before he was alive?

A contradiction. Impossible to imagine his or, for that matter, her own nonexistence.

* * *

Yet an astrophysicist—an astrophysicist like Lorna—would know how to exist in abstract spaces, spaces with completely different geometrical properties that extend the methods of vector algebra and calculus and the two-dimensional Euclidean plane to ones with any finite or infinite number of dimensions. Hilbert space, momentum space, reciprocal space, phase space.

Spaces Nina knows nothing about.

There.

There she is!

Nina envisions curly-haired Lorna, with her skinny arms covered with freckles spread out in a perfect T, expertly navigating her way in the blinding space in which Uranus and Neptune orbit around the sun—she who did not know how to drive a car!—wearing the mismatched ballet flats: the one silver, the other black.

She is impervious to the cold—the temperature on Neptune averages minus 218 degrees Centigrade.

She is impervious to the wind—the winds on Neptune blow up to 2,100 kilometers an hour.

Yet Lorna manages to stay serenely aloft and steer her appointed course. And, oh, the blue. Lorna marvels at the color of the two planets. Never in her whole life could she have imagined such vibrant colors! The result, she knows all too well, of the absorption of red light by the atmospheric methane in the outermost regions of the planets. At the same time, she cannot help noticing that Neptune's blue is a brighter, richer blue than the blue of Uranus, which she is tempted to describe as

aquamarine. Her mother, she has just enough memory to remember, wore an aquamarine ring and the stone, she claimed,
came from a country in South America. Peru. But she must
not let herself become distracted by unscientific thoughts. The
planet's aquamarine color could be the result of an as yet unknown atmospheric constituent.

If only she had the time to discover what that constituent
might be.

She wishes she could linger here on Uranus; spend a summer day that could last several years or sleep for a night that
lasts longer.

The thought of it makes Lorna yawn.

And if only Lorna could describe those blues, or paint them.

Nina blinks then opens her eyes wide.

Was she dreaming?

She must have fallen asleep.

The image of Lorna in space lingers in her head.

Round and round she will go, always returning to her starting point, since Lorna believes in a finite universe.

Nina is tempted to wave to her.

To say *bon voyage*.

Philip and Nina talk of returning to Angangueo but they never
have. Instead, one year, as an anniversary present, Nina paints
Philip a watercolor of six butterflies on handmade Japanese

mulberry paper. She copies the butterflies from a book of photographs. At first, she had thought to paint only one butterfly,
the monarch, but, absorbed by the photos, she decides to paint
more.

She begins with a solar ellipse, a yellow butterfly, the color
of an Italian lemon, with orange flame spots on its wings; the
second butterfly, an aurora, is electric blue with purple streaks on
its wings; the third is transparent—except for a deep rose blush
on the lower part of its wings—and so delicate that Nina holds
her breath while she colors it on the page; she places the orange
monarch, the biggest butterfly, in the center of the watercolor
and paints the white dots and splashes on its wings using the
tip of her best sable brush; the fifth butterfly is a garish green-
and-orange-and-pink-and-yellow-and-black sunset moth. *A moth,*
Nina reads, *flies at night while the butterfly flies during the day; the
moth rests with its wings clapped horizontally on its body while the
butterfly rests with its vertically.* . . . The last butterfly, a silver satyr
from Chile, is the color of shiny Christmas tinsel, with a wash
of cocoa brown on the tips of its serrated wings, and is the most
starkly beautiful.

The colors are lovely, Philip says. He sounds genuinely
pleased.

In real life, the colors are brighter, Nina says.

The blues and greens are instances of iridescence, Philip
adds.

The watercolor hangs in Philip's office and he has repeatedly
assured Nina that should his office catch on fire, the first thing

he would grab to save from the flames—not his computer, not his precious papers—is her butterflies.

She would like to believe him.

Nina rarely visits Philip at work unannounced, but not so long ago—the memory of it still makes her blush—she recalls knocking on his office door, then, not waiting for an answer, opening it. Philip is talking on the phone.

Isabelle Theo—she does not quite catch the last name, a foreign-sounding one—makes my life a lot easier, Nina hears him say.

Raising his free hand, Philip frowns and makes a sign for her to wait.

I don't know what I would do, he also says, as he swivels his chair away from his desk, turning his back on Nina, before he finished his sentence and hangs up the phone and swivels his chair back around to face her.

Are you okay? he asks. I wasn't expecting you.

I was in Cambridge having lunch. I thought I would stop by on my way home, Nina answers.

I have a class in a minute, Philip says, looking up at the wall clock in his office.

Isabelle who? Nina asks, keeping her voice even. A secretary? A student?

Isabelle?

Is Philip feigning ignorance?

Oh—he starts to laugh. Do you want to meet her?

Look. Philip motions for Nina to come around as he points to his computer screen.

Isabelle is a software program. A generic theorem prover. It allows mathematical and computer science formulas to be expressed in a formal language. It comes with a large library of formally verified mathematics, including elementary number theory, set theory, the basic properties of limits, derivatives, and integrals—shall I go on?

Nina shakes her head.

An art teacher once told Nina to stop painting from her hand and wrist, and to paint from her shoulder. He advised her to work only in charcoal. Charcoal, he said, is simple, cheap, and connects the artist to the earth. And Nina should try to forget what she has learned—checking angles, calculating perspective—and, instead, learn to work quickly, almost blindly, and follow her instinct. She has to trust that somewhere between her shoulder and the paper an image will appear.

She has to give herself more room, stand farther back.

At first, she draws nothing but loops. Big loops. Some of them are so thick and dark that at times she presses too hard and the charcoal breaks off; others are lighter, the lines smudged, shades spread across the paper.

Drawing loops makes her feel exercised. The way she used to feel in the early mornings after she had run a couple of miles.

Or when she dances.

Or how she might feel if she could sing.

*   *   *

Again, she looks over at Philip, lying next to her.

To herself, she tries to hum a few lines from *La vie en rose*.

Has she kept the charcoal portraits she did of Philip?

Or did she throw them out?

She can get the flashlight from the shelf in the hall closet downstairs, cross the garden—the grass will be wet from the rain—and go to her studio and look for them.

The sketches were not bad.

But she does not want to leave Philip.

What time is it?

Leaning over Philip, she tries to read the hands on the clock.

The numbers are blurry.

4:20? 4:40?

The hand that sets off the alarm is in the way.

Philip does not wear a watch.

From time to time, he has tried. He buys himself a cheap watch—a Timex or a Casio—but either he loses the watch or the watch stops working.

It must have something to do with my circadian rhythm, he says.

Nonsense, it's the cheap watch, Nina tells him.

Nevertheless, Philip—unless he is held up at work—is rarely late. He has an uncanny ability to tell the time.

What time is it, Dad? Louise, as a child, likes to test him.

12:35.

Wrong! Louise shouts. 12:25.

Your watch is slow, Lulu, Philip tells her.

And, anyway, he continues, there is no absolute time. According to Einstein, each individual has his own personal measure of time, which depends on where he is and how he is moving.

Louise rolls her eyes at him.

If you had a twin, Lulu, and you were to go up in a spaceship at the speed of light for a few light-years and then return to earth to rejoin your twin, which of you would be younger? Philip goes on to ask her. You or your twin?

Of course, Nina knows the answer.

Like Iris, the spaceship twin is still young and beautiful while the twin left behind on earth, like her, is wrinkled and gray.

She starts to shut her eyes and opens them quickly.

Dizzy again.

Nauseated.

* * *

When did she last eat?

A sandwich at lunch while she paints sky and sea—part of the triptych.

The painting, she decides, is flat. Too cool.

She adds a coat of white and sands it back, a coat of yellow and sands that back, another coat of white to which she adds a little cerulean, then she sands that back as well. She has to build up a surface. She has to make it dense.

Eventually, she promises herself, she will make the painting work.

She will have to throw his ashes into the sea.

Louise will come with her.

They will remember to stand to leeward so that the ashes won't blow back in their faces.

In the Musée du Jeu de Paume one afternoon, Nina asks Philip, Who is your favorite artist?

In the world?

Yes, in the world.

You.

No, seriously.

Cézanne. Yes, Cézanne.

They are standing in front of his self-portrait.

Cézanne is everyone's favorite artist, Nina says a little impatiently.

Look at the self-assured way he stares out from the painting. His gaze is hypnotic, Philip says, ignoring her remark and
gesturing to the portrait. I'm tempted to grow a beard just like
his, he also says.

Don't, Nina says.

Laughing, they move on.

Outside, it has begun to rain; neither one of them has brought
an umbrella. Lightning flashes in bright succession followed
by claps of thunder as they hurry to cross the Place de la
Concorde and the Pont de la Concorde and run up boulevard
Saint-Germain to the nearest café. They are both soaked.

At the bar, Philip orders them each a glass of Armagnac.

The expensive liquor burns her throat and makes her
cough.

I think I'm falling in love with you, Philip tells her.

Still coughing, she shakes her head, then once she stops,
she laughs as she catches sight of herself in the bar mirror—
her wet hair is plastered to her skull, black mascara streaks her
cheeks.

After a pause, Philip says, Do you play tennis?

Why? Nina asks. Is that your criterion for falling in love?

Yes, Philip answers.

I do. I'm pretty good, she says.

In spite of his limp—on the court, it all but disappears—Philip
plays well. He is tall and has a long reach; at net, few balls get
past him. Once a week, at eight thirty on Tuesday mornings, he

has a standing appointment to play men's doubles. He plays indoors on a clay court and none of the four men he plays with is a mathematician. Nothing can deter Philip from going to his weekly tennis game.

He played two days ago, Nina recollects.

We won again, he tells her when he gets home. We are invincible, he says and laughs.

I served a couple of aces, he also boasts.

Philip puts a spin on his serve that makes the ball bounce high and out of his opponent's reach.

"If the score in a tennis game reaches deuce, what is the probability that the server will win the next two points?" is one of the problems he poses his students in class. No one answers. "You all play tennis, don't you?" Philip asks. "You know how the scoring works—when the two players reach a tie, which in tennis is called deuce, one player has to win the game by two successive points. Since there is no limit to the number of deuces in a game," he continues, "the problem may appear infinite but it's not."

Fault, Nina says out loud.

They always argue on the tennis court.

Out, out, the ball was out, she shouts at him.

No way, Philip shouts back as he walks to the net and peers over it to where his serve landed. It was in. You must be blind.

With her racket, Nina points to a mark outside the line. The ball landed here. See.

I don't see anything. You're lying.

Cheater, she yells.

"Trust me." Smiling, Philip turns around to address the class. "In tennis, the server always has the advantage. A strong server especially." Stepping away from the blackboard, Philip stretches out his arm as if holding an imaginary racket and mimes tossing a ball into the air, then swings.

When they step out of the café, the sky is a clear blue again, the only signs that it has rained are the wet, shiny pavement and the orderly streams of water running into the street gutters. Nina's hair is dry, her face is washed clean. She feels a little light-headed from the brandy as they make their way up the boulevard toward Tante Thea's apartment.

Before they reach rue de Saint-Simon, Philip stops at a tabac and buys a pack of Gauloise cigarettes, then he takes Nina by the hand as if he is leading her to some unfamiliar but important place.

This time when he comes back from playing tennis, Philip remembers to put his white tennis shorts, polo shirt, and socks in the laundry hamper.

And, yesterday, Marta must have taken them out and washed them.

* * *

She hugs herself.

She is still wearing Philip's old yellow windbreaker.

Then, holding up her hands, she twirls the wedding ring on her finger.

Sailing off the coast of Belle-Île one windy summer afternoon, Philip lets go of the tiller for a moment to pull off his ring. The ring is tight on his finger and he has to twist it round and round before he can get it off. Then, frowning, he says something that because of the wind she cannot hear and throws the ring as far out as he can into the sea. Rudderless, the boat has come around and is headed into the wind, the sails are flapping noisily. He is in irons.

No, not true—she is making this up.

She slept with Jean-Marc only three or four times. Not enough to qualify as a proper affair.

Instead, one hand on the tiller, Philip is eating a peach with the other. The peach is ripe and sweet and the juice drips down Philip's fingers. When he finishes it, he throws the pit into the sea, then, leaning far over the side of the boat, he dips his sticky fingers overboard to rinse them. The water is unexpectedly cold and the ring slips off his finger. Helplessly, Philip watches as it shimmies for an instant in the dark blue water, then the gold ring disappears. A second later, a silver fish with spiny dorsal fins swims by so fast that Philip catches only a glimpse of it—a large sea bass, he guesses, weighing at least ten or twelve pounds. The fish gives a flick of its tail fin as it dives down after the ring, its ugly mouth already open and set to swallow it.

* * *

In their Volkswagen with over eighty-thousand miles on it, she drives Jean-Marc to Buzzards Bay; he has an appointment to talk to the director of the sailing school. While she waits for him, she walks aimlessly around the New England town, looking through the shop windows and looking at her watch.

I want to examine the programs here, he says to her, in the car, in his accented English.

Her eyes fixed on the road, she nods.

En français, she tells him.

She is awkward with him.

Non, non, I must practice in English, Jean-Marc answers.

He is awkward with her.

Except for greeting him with a kiss on both cheeks when he walked through the front door, she has not touched him. Nor has he her. In his suit, dress shirt, and tie, Jean-Marc looks shorter and no longer like himself or the way Nina remembers him in his jeans.

Or taking them off.

She shakes her head to dispel the memory.

Ma chérie is what Philip calls her.

What does Jean-Marc call her?

Ni*na*—he puts the accent on the second syllable, making her name unfamiliar.

A few years after the summer of Nina's affair with him, Jean-Marc comes to stay for a few days—days he wants to spend investigating New England sailing schools.

On Saturday, Philip suggests they drive to Marblehead.

A perfect day for an outing. We can have lunch and walk around, he says to persuade Nina and Louise.

A historic New England town, Philip tells Jean-Marc in the car, founded in the early 1600s.

Up until the midnineteenth century, it was an important fishing port and commercial center, Philip continues. Now, it's become more of a seaside resort with large summer homes.

Like Belle-Île, Jean-Marc says.

Together, he and Philip walk around the harbor inspecting the boats; Nina and Louise trail along behind them. A slight wind rattles the halyards on the masts; gulls wheel and cry overhead.

Ma chérie, Philip whispers to her, after they make love the second time in Tante Thea's apartment.

Philip wears a faded red polo shirt and khakis; he is a head taller than Jean-Marc.

In the restaurant on the wharf, they order lobster rolls for lunch.

Too much mayonnaise, Jean-Marc complains. However, he eats two. He sits next to Louise in the booth, and, putting his hand on her arm, he offers her some of the French fries that come with the lobster roll.

Louise picks at her salad and shakes her head.

You should eat, he tells her. You're too thin.

Louise shrugs. She is fifteen.

After lunch, they visit a historic mansion. The guide speaks with a Boston accent and tells them about the silver collection, the fall-front mahogany desk made by a local cabinetmaker, the banjo clock, a painted rocking chair.

Do you understand what she is saying? Philip asks Jean-Marc.

Bien sûr, he answers.

Nina stands close to Louise, avoiding Jean-Marc.

On the way home, in the car, Jean-Marc insists on sitting in the back, next to Louise.

Louise, Louise.

Asleep now, Nina imagines, in the arms of the handsome young man.

Tall, thin, athletic, lovely Louise.

As a teenager, she is too thin. Skinny.

She hardly eats anything, Nina complains to Philip.

She says she's a vegetarian.

Leave her alone. The more you badger her about food, the less she'll eat, Philip says.

What if she becomes anorexic?

Lulu is too competitive to starve herself.

Competitive with whom? Nina asks.

Calm, polite, reasonable is how she always describes Philip.

Intelligent, too, of course.

Even brilliant.

And tall.

Under the quilt, she guesses at the outline of his long, thin legs—the left one has a lump in the middle of it, where the tibia did not set properly—that reach to the foot of the bed.

Again, she reaches over and touches his cheek.
Leaning down, she kisses him gently.
Her lips barely brush his skin.
Tears well up in her eyes.

Red is Philip's favorite color. If he had his way, everything in the house would be red: the furniture, the curtains, the walls, all covered and painted red.
His car, another Volkswagen, is red.
Colors exist to provoke desire, he likes to say.
She is certain that he is quoting someone.
She glances over at the closet where the red silk coat he brought her back from Hong Kong hangs in plastic.

Careful not to disturb him, she gets out of bed. In the dark, she feels among her clothes until she gets to the coat and she takes down the hanger. Tearing off the plastic, she undoes the silk frog buttons and slips her arms into the roomy sleeves; she wears the coat over the windbreaker. Inside the closet door, in the mirror, she glimpses herself—too dark to make out the embroidered blue and green peonies—a vague shiny shape. Then she climbs back into bed and lies down next to Philip.

See, she tells him, smoothing out the stiff red silk so that it spreads in tidy folds around her, I'm wearing it now.

Am I desirable? she is tempted to ask.

In her tight-fitting silk *qipao*, Sofia leads Philip into another room, where her collection of antique blue-and-white Ming bowls is neatly aligned on a shelf.

Beautiful, he says, picking up a bowl—the transparent one with the rough-looking mark.

Careful, Sofia warns him.

But he drops it.

Sofia lets out a little yelp of alarm.

The same little yelp.

Nina has never been to Hong Kong.

Or to Asia.

Bangkok, Chiang Mai, she likes to think, and Siem Reap, where she will watch the sunrise from Angkor Wat, then Luang Prabang.

Luang Prabang, she repeats to herself.

She likes the sound of the words—like candy or a sweet dessert.

It will be hot and she will pack light, cotton skirts and T-shirts, she can handwash, comfortable sandals she and Philip can take on and off easily when they visit Wat Arun, the temple made out of broken dishes, when they climb the 309 steps leading up to Wat Phrathat Doi Suthep, or when they hike through the jungle in search of Banteay Samré and Ta Prohm, the temples left unrestored and enveloped by giant banyan trees—

She and Philip often talk about this trip.

I'd like to go up the Mekong by boat, Philip says. The river is about two thousand miles long—the longest in Southeast Asia—and drains an area of about three hundred thousand square miles, discharging 114 cubic . . .

Her eyes closed, she sees herself on the deck of the boat as they sail past agile young men, throwing out their fishing nets from the banks of the river, past dark-haired women dressed in colorful sarongs, squatting on the raised decks of their wooden houses, cooking their spicy midday meal, and past naked children splashing and waving at them from the dirty brown water; occasionally a plastic bag floats by or, worse, a bloated dead animal.

She looks around the boat for Philip.

Where is he?

She must not forget to pack a hat.

With the guidebook, she fans herself.

Hot.

For her thirty-ninth birthday, Philip gives her a large-brimmed red straw hat.

Redheads aren't supposed to—she starts to tell him but he interrupts her.

Redheads should always wear red, he says.

In his office, on his desk, there is a framed color photo of her sitting in her two-piece bathing suit on the beach at Belle-Île; she is wearing the red hat.

Is that your wife? people must ask him.

When was the picture taken? How long ago?

And where was it taken? Abroad somewhere?

Next to it, there is a more recent photo of Louise. A black-and-white formal portrait.

My daughter, Louise, Philip tells them.

Once again, she gets out of bed.

What would Philip say if he could see her walking uncertainly around the bedroom, dressed like a clown?

Would he laugh?

She goes to the window and opens it.

The cool air feels good on her face.

The sky is filled with stars—late night stars she cannot identify.

No doubt Philip can.

She thinks of Lorna spinning around them.

What does she say that night at dinner? Something about how we humans are created from the same basic substance as the universe, how we are made from the same material as the stars.

Lorna is eating a slice of the pineapple upside-down cake.

She and Philip are talking about Einstein—about Einstein's ultimate theory of everything—and, midsentence, Philip interrupts himself to say, Someone once told Einstein that, to an astronomer, man is nothing but an insignificant dot in an infinite universe.

And you know what Einstein replied? Philip asks.

Her mouth full of cake, Lorna shakes her head.

That may be true, but the insignificant dot is also an astronomer.

Lorna laughs, then, turning to Nina, says, This cake is delicious. Can you give me the recipe?

In the bathroom, Nina avoids looking at herself in the mirror.

Then she goes back and lies down on the bed.

Cautiously, she shuts her eyes.

Soon it will be daylight and morning.

Often, as soon as she awakes and before she forgets them, she tells Philip her dreams—vivid dreams that make no sense—and, less often—for as soon as he opens his eyes he claims to have forgotten them—he tells her his.

Dreams, Philip says, are generated in the brain stem and are meaningless until the dreamer transforms them to suit his or her own personal characteristics.

Nina disagrees. Dreams, she says, are motivated by desires.

Last night I dreamt about a dog, Nina tells him. A big black-and-white mutt—a mix between a German shepherd and some other breed. I was walking the dog when all of a sudden the street I was on, a vaguely familiar-looking street—familiar, perhaps, because I recognized it from an earlier dream—turned into a giant dump or landfill and the dog was straining at the leash trying to—

Funny, Philip interrupts, now I remember. I dreamt about walking a dog, too, last night. My dog, Natty Bumppo, I think.

What was the dog doing?

I don't know. I don't remember.

Maybe we had the same dream, Nina says.

Maybe, Philip answers.

Dr. Mayer urges her to write down her dreams.

During one of their sessions, Nina starts to tell Dr. Mayer about the recurring nightmare she had as a child—the one about the ever increasing numbers and how Philip has said that the dream stands for the terror of the infinite—but Dr. Mayer, she guesses, knows nothing about infinity.

Instead, she makes up a dream about a house. A large elegant house made entirely out of glass. A house unlike any other she has ever seen or been in. However, the moment she opens the front door and steps inside, she knows that she has come home.

This house is home—home for the past twenty years.

And this bed, too—she pats the quilt for emphasis.

The bed, an antique four-poster, was propped up on its side and covered in dust and bird droppings inside a barn that sold used lumber and farm equipment.

The headboard is hand-carved, the owner, a farmer, told her, spitting tobacco juice into a can. Six hundred dollars. Not a penny less.

Look at the cracks. The frame needs a lot of work, Nina argued back.

She had bargained him down to four hundred and fifty dollars. At the time, it was a fortune.

And how many nights have she and Philip slept in the bed?

How many hours?

"Take for example," Philip tells his first-year students, "that, on average, my wife and I sleep eight hours each night. However, this is not always true"—a student in the back row gives a snort of laughter. "The reason being," Philip continues, ignoring the student, "we have a newborn baby. Her name is Louise and, during the day Louise smiles and coos, but at night Louise is transformed into a different baby altogether, a baby who does nothing but cry"—a few students, most of them women, laugh—"and either me or my wife has to get out of bed and go change and feed her, which means that we may only get five or six hours of sleep a night. But as we have seen"—here, Philip turns his back to the class and starts to draw on the blackboard—"the normal distribution, known as the Gaussian distribution, will show us how, at least approximately, any variable—the nights my wife and I don't get to sleep eight hours—tends to cluster around the mean, which is that glorious night of eight hours of uninterrupted sleep when Louise does not cry—"

Nina stops eating dairy—coffee ice cream, an afterdinner treat—along with onions, cabbage, cauliflower, vegetables she does not much care for but that give her gas. She gives up caffeine—her morning coffee—all the better to breast-feed Louise.

Colic, pure and simple.

Month after month, Louise cries every night. For hours, Nina rocks Louise in the rocking chair; she gives her a warm bath but, in the tub, Louise only cries harder, she is inconsolable. Exhausted, Nina puts on her coat over her nightgown, hauls the bassinet with Louise in it, still crying, down the three flights of stairs—again, the dog in the apartment below them barks and his owner yells *Shut up, damn it*—and she puts Louise in the backseat of the car. Except for the streetlights and for an occasional shout from a bar open late, the streets are dark and quiet as, slowly, tentatively, holding the wheel tightly in both hands, Nina drives through Cambridge, Mt. Auburn, and Watertown. Once she drives as far as Waltham before Louise finally stops crying and falls asleep.

At night, Nina begins to hate Louise.

Natty Bumppo, the black-and-white German shepherd mix, in her dream, was straining so hard on the leash that the leash broke. She chased after him, calling out—

Tobias—without thinking about it, she remembers the name of the neighbors' old yellow Lab.

Stiff and a little uncomfortable, she shifts her weight carefully on the bed.

She does not want to disturb Philip or wrinkle the red silk coat.

*　*　*

Aboard *Hypatia*, in a sudden gust, the red straw hat blows off her head and into the water.

Oh, she cries. My hat!

Too bad. Philip shakes his head.

Come about, she pleads, let me try and get it.

Already, she has gotten the boat hook and is hurrying up to the bow.

Ready about, Philip yells.

I'll come up alongside it to starboard, he also says.

Lying flat on her stomach on the boat's deck in the bow and holding out the boat hook, Nina leans as far over the side as she dares, watching the red hat, bobbing up and down in the water, as it comes closer, and determined—even if she falls overboard—to grab it.

Faded, the straw broken and frayed along the brim, the red hat hangs from a nail on the wall of her studio. Next to it hangs her painting of it floating in the water. In charcoal, at the bottom among the waves, she has scrawled: *el sombrero cayó en el agua.*

A joke.

According to her mother, *el sombrero cayó en el agua* were the first words Nina, as a child, learns to say in Spanish.

Sombrrrerrro—she repeats to herself, rolling the Rs.

Why? she wonders.

Did her hat fall in the water?
Or was it her twin Linda's hat?

Padre Nuestro, que estás en los cielos. . . .
    At one time, she could recite the Lord's Prayer in Spanish.
Later, she learns it in French:
    Notre Père, qui es aux cieux . . .
    A superstitious child, she never steps on a crack, yet she
does not believe in a God.
    Now she is not sure.
    Our Father who art. . . .

She should toss a coin.
    Heads? God is.
    Tails? He is not.
    She should not have drunk so much wine.

Philip believes that the universe had a beginning. Once there
was nothing and now there is a lot. But this, he says, has nothing to do with God.
    How do you mean there was nothing? Nina asks.
    I mean nothing.
    Air? Space?
    No. Nothing.
    I can't imagine it.
    No one can.

                         *   *   *

She shuts her eyes.

Nothing is like nonexistence.

Like death.

But what if God created the big bang? What if God made the universe make itself? For argument's sake, Nina asks.

That would satisfy a lot of people who believe in the story of Genesis. Pass me another crêpe, please, and the jam. Not apricot, the other kind, Philip says.

Myrtille.

She and Philip are the last ones having breakfast in the dining room. A waitress is clearing the dishes off the other tables and heaping them noisily on a tray.

Encore deux cafés, s'il vous plaît, Philip calls out.

She wants us to leave, Nina says, nervous, glancing over at the waitress.

The day before, they take the train from Paris to Brest, and from Brest, a bus to Ploudalmézeau, where they rent bicycles. From there, in the driving rain, they bike the thirteen kilometers to the village of Tréglonou.

I'm sopping wet, Nina complains when they stop by the side of the road so that Philip can study the map.

We must have missed the turn, he says.

Let's ask someone, Nina suggests as a car speeds past.

I know where we are. It must just be a few hundred meters back down this road. Let's turn around and keep going.

Back and forth they ride down narrow roads bordered by

wet green fields, where bunches of horses and cows are huddled together against the rain. Wait, wait, Nina wails to herself as she pedals behind Philip. She is wearing a long skirt and the hem catches in the spokes of the bicycle wheel, twice she has almost fallen off. Philip does not appear to notice.

In the village of Plouvien, Nina stops to hike up her skirt. Across the street, a priest in a long black cassock is locking the door to a church, then, turning, he opens his large black umbrella. When he sees Nina straddling her bicycle by the side of the road, he walks over and asks her if she needs his help.

This morning, it is still raining.

But I thought you said you believe in God, Nina says.

I believe in a libertarian God. A God who allows room for free will, Philip says, yawning. I wish we could go back to bed, he also says, taking Nina's hand and bringing it to his lips.

Nina smiles. Are you saying that God can't predict the future?

Let me describe another possibility, Philip says, rearranging the plates on the table as, frowning, the waitress brings them more coffee.

Merci, madame, Nina says.

Let us suppose that I order two breakfasts. This one, he points to his plate, is a classic breakfast: a crêpe with *myrtille* jam or a crêpe with apricot jam, the other, the quantum breakfast, he says, taking Nina's empty plate, is a crêpe and a superposition with both *myrtille* and apricot jam.

Nina shakes her head. A superposition of—

The superposition principle states that if the world can be in any configuration and also in another configuration, then the world can also be in a state that is a superposition of the two. In other words, the God-created universe and the big-bang-created universe can coexist. By using the mathematics of partial existence, we can think critically about both theology and physics. Or, to use my example, I can eat my *myrtille* and apricot jam breakfast at the same time.

I haven't understood a thing you've said, Nina says.

Finish your crêpe—the classic one—and, look, she tells him, it's stopped raining.

Ploudalmézeau, Tréglonou—*ou, ou*—she pushes out her lips to form the syllables as, silently, she practices pronouncing those Celtic names.

B.B.B. and A.B.B. is how we divide cosmic time, Philip also tells her that morning at breakfast. B.B.B. stands for before the big bang, the way B.C. stands for before Jesus Christ, and A.B.B., of course, stands for after the big bang.

Of course.

All day the sun tries to shine through the heavy, low gray clouds. Occasionally, for a few bright moments, it succeeds, shedding an intense light over the flat countryside that makes the grass look greener, the sea bluer, a field of cauliflowers sparkle like diamonds.

Chou-fleur, she says to herself.

Myrtille.

Across the road, the cows and horses stand sharply outlined.

I should have brought a hat, Nina says, shading her eyes. She wears jeans and has no trouble keeping up with Philip as they ride toward the coast.

Then it begins to rain again—not the heavy downpour of the day before but a light drizzle.

Let's stop and have lunch, Philip says.

We just finished breakfast, she answers.

It must be the sea air. I'm hungry again, Philip says.

In Landéda, they eat more crêpes—crêpes coquilles St.-Jacques this time.

And drink homemade cider.

Nina licks her lips; she is thirsty.

In the bathroom, without turning on the light, she pours herself a glass of water.

The water will clear her head.

Too cold to swim and, anyway, they did not bring bathing suits.

No one's on the beach, we could just take off our clothes and run in, Philip says.

Already he has kicked off his shoes and is taking off his shirt, unzipping his trousers.

Come on, he shouts to her.

*   *   *

I MARRIED YOU FOR HAPPINESS

Back in bed, Nina shivers.

Frigid, the water takes her breath away.

She swims a few strokes, then quickly turns back to shore.

That was a test, Philip tells her as he comes out of the water.

Shivering, her back to him, Nina tries to dry herself with her clothes. A test for what? she asks.

Nina, he calls to her softly.

Turning, she starts to say, What—

Naked, Philip is on his knees in the sand. Will you marry me? he asks.

On their way back to Tréglonou, it starts to rain again; then, all of a sudden, the sun breaks through the clouds and, directly in front of them—at their feet almost—a rainbow.

Make a wish, Nina tells Philip.

No need, Philip answers as he begins to sing:

Anything can happen on a summer afternoon
On a lazy dazy golden hazy summer afternoon

As they bicycle past a field, a dappled gray horse stops grazing and, raising his head, pricks up his ears to listen to Philip.

I can't believe Dad proposed to you naked, Louise says.

And you were naked, too.

I had on my underwear, Nina tells her.

* * *

In the car, late at night, as she is driving Louise through the
Boston suburbs to get her to go to sleep, a policeman in a patrol
car, flashing his blue lights, makes her pull over.

You went through a stop sign, he tells her.

A ticket already in hand, he stands by the car window.

Can I see your license?

In her hurry, Nina has forgotten to bring her purse.

Officer, I can—she tries to explain when, in the backseat,
Louise begins to cry.

Can you step out of the car, please.

Under her coat, Nina's nightgown trails to the ground; on
her feet, she wears bedroom slippers.

Ma'am—the policeman starts to say.

Okay, go on home, he says instead.

How did their argument start?

On their way home from dinner—Philip is at the wheel—Nina
made a remark about how much Louise is spending on her new
condominium on Russian Hill, only she does not remember it.

It is during the Christmas holidays.

And I don't see why you need a decorator.

Mom, it's none of your business what I spend on a decorator or on furniture or, for that matter, on my bathroom fixtures.
I want the place to look good.

I know, Louise, but don't you think there's a limit?

A limit to what?

Well, just as I said, to spending money, especially when one thinks about how people in the rest of the world—

Mom, give me a break, Louise says. I don't see you making huge lifestyle changes to accommodate how people in the rest of the world live.

I try to volunteer—

Just so you know, I make a lot of money and I have the right to decide how to spend it, Louise interrupts.

Hey, ladies, can you keep it down a little, Philip says. I'm trying to drive.

I'm serious, Louise continues, turning her attention to Philip. I am thirty-two years old and I don't see what business she has telling me how I should spend the money I work hard making.

The three are silent for a few minutes.

Furthermore, Louise starts up again, addressing Nina this time, it's not as if you ever made any money of your own, Mom.

Lulu, Philip says.

It's okay, Nina says. Let her say what she wants. And for your information, Louise, I was working when I met your father and I have also sold quite a number of my paintings.

Yeah, yeah, to your friends, Louise says.

No one speaks.

You're being rude and unkind to your mother, Philip says finally.

She is tempted to laugh.

Philip's shrunken penis is all but hidden in the thick bush of his pubic hair as, thin, naked, and wet, he kneels in front of her on the beach.

Ploudalmézeau, Tréglonou—again, she mouths the names.

You'll catch cold, she tells him.

Is that your answer? he asks.

Yes, she says.

Yes.

Naked is to be oneself and nude is to be seen naked by others, Nina says, to convince Philip to take off his clothes while she is doing his portrait.

Nudity is to be put on display, she also says.

I am not sure I want to be put on display, Philip says.

If you look at European paintings of nudes—Ingres' *La Grande Odalisque*, for example, Nina continues, warming up to her subject, and look at the way the model stares out from the canvas, it is clear that she is aware that someone is looking at her, admiring and desiring her. The nude in the portrait is both the compliant object and the seductress.

What about nakedness?

Nakedness is you and me taking off our clothes before we go to bed at night. Nakedness has no disguises, nakedness has no surprises.

I haven't smoked in years, Philip says, but all of a sudden I really want a cigarette.

You surprised me, Philip tells her after they make love in Tante Thea's apartment on rue de Saint-Simon Your body. Somehow, I pictured it differently.

Differently how? Nina asks him.

Fatter?

No, not fatter. Just different.

Can you be more specific?

Not as beautiful, Philip says.

It snowed the day before but the narrow country road they are driving on has been plowed and is clear. As they turn a corner, the car headlights pick up two deer eating the salt by the side of the road. Startled, the deer raise their heads and start to run across the road.

Damn, Philip says as he applies the brakes.

Swerving into the other lane, the car lurches to a stop as the first deer disappears into the woods and as, behind it, the second deer just manages to clear the car's front fender.

Nina lets out her breath but does not say anything.

That was close, Philip says, once they are back on the right-hand side of the road.

Is everyone okay? he also asks, glancing toward the backseat.

Did you have your seat belt on? he asks Louise.

I couldn't find it, she says. I landed on the floor, she adds, settling herself again on the backseat and rubbing her knee.

How old is this car? she asks. Isn't it time you bought a new one?

For a while no one says anything as Philip slowly drives on.

Oh, and, Dad, your windbreaker, Louise mumbles. Don't you have a decent-looking jacket? It's embarrassing.

Lulu, honey, this happens to be my favorite jacket. If your mother ever decided to throw it out, I'd leave her.

They are silent during the rest of the drive home.

Once in the house, Nina goes straight upstairs, without saying good night to either Louise or Philip.

She undresses and gets into bed. Too agitated to sleep, she waits for Philip.

At dinner, did Louise drink too much?

Where did all the anger come from?

Downstairs, late into the night and until, finally, in spite of herself, she falls asleep, Nina can hear laughter. What, she wonders, are they doing?

Tossing pennies?

Whatever it is, Philip and Louise have forgotten about her and Philip has forgotten Louise's harsh words.

In her dream that night, Nina conflates the deer crossing the road with Iris.

Soon, it will be light.

Depending on how it is observed, light is both a wave and a particle—this much she knows for certain.

* * *

The next morning, at breakfast, Louise apologizes.

If you can bring yourself to forgive me, Mom, she says, I would love to have one of your paintings to hang in my apartment. I'll give it pride of place in the living room.

Yes, of course, Nina answers, putting down her coffee cup. I am honored—only it will cost you.

In her portrait of him wearing red boxer shorts, Philip is holding a cigarette in his hand.

A Gauloise Bleue.

Nina opens her mouth and exhales loudly as if exhaling smoke.

Shutting her eyes, she slowly runs her hands down along her body—a body, covered in the red silk coat and Philip's old nylon windbreaker, that she can hardly feel and that does not feel like hers.

How long ago everything seems to her.

And how unreal.

She cannot imagine a life without Philip.

Nor does she want to.

Philip is young, good looking, and they are about to meet.

Vous permettez? he asks, pointing to the empty chair at her table.

Je vous en prie, she shrugs, without looking up at him.

What is your book about? he asks her after a while.

Again she shrugs.

Hard to explain, she says, not looking at him. It's about trying to capture and transform into language the manifestations of the inner self, the vibrations and the tremors of feelings on the threshold of consciousness. In other words, the book is an attempt to try to put into words what essentially is nonverbal communication.

Sounds like a thankless task, Philip says.

Already, she is in love with him.

A love that has not yet manifested itself on the threshold of her consciousness.

A love whose vibrations and tremors she cannot yet feel; a love it will take her some time to become aware of.

And put into words.

In the meantime, she will resist him.

And, so far, she has barely glanced at him. If she were asked, she would have a hard time describing him: tall? dark-haired? a nice voice.

She is scarcely civil.

He raises his arm to get the attention of the waiter.

Are you a student? he also asks.

No, she replies.

You're French, right?

No, she says again.

He laughs.

I am not either.

She looks up at him.

Where are you from? he asks.

All over, she says. Most recently, Massachusetts.

Me, too, he says.

What are you doing in Paris?

Do you want another coffee? he asks.

Deux cafés crème, he tells the waiter before she can answer him.

Outside, in the garden, she hears birds chirping.

She takes only a small sip of the *café crème* he has ordered for her.

She does not want to be beholden to him.

Too much caffeine, she tells him. It might give me a migraine.

You get migraines? he says, sounding concerned.

Already she has divulged too much. She does not yet want his sympathy.

They must be terrible but the good news is that they're working on a new group of drugs that constrict the blood vessels in the brain and may prove to be very effective for relieving migraines.

Are you a doctor?

A mathematician, he says. And you, what do you do?

She hesitates.

I paint.

* * *

How do you approach a painting? Philip asks while he is posing for her in his boxer shorts. I don't mean a portrait. That's obvious.

Do you know what the painting will look like when you finish it? he continues. I am interested in the process—how people create. How it applies to mathematicians as well.

I start with a line, a color, and then I look for something else—it's hard to describe what exactly, Nina answers.

Is it random? Do you just stumble accidentally on whatever it is?

Sometimes. But, no, not always.

Stand still, she also tells him.

She is painting his long legs, exaggerating how thin and long they are, like a Giacometti sculpture, making the lump larger in the left one.

I read somewhere that art is about navigating the space between what you know and what you see, Philip says.

I look for clarity, Nina tells him.

In a class Philip once took, Richard Feynman described the size of an atom by telling his students to think of an apple magnified to the size of the earth, then the atoms inside the apple are the approximate size of the original apple.

Clarity.

For a dollar, Nina sells Louise one of the near-monochrome *Migraine* paintings and, as promised, Louise hangs it on the living room wall of her new Russian Hill apartment. Most of Louise's furniture is modern, stark, and white, and Nina's red painting stands in sharp contrast.

It looks great, like a Rothko, Louise tells her mother.

How will she tell Louise?

What will she say?

I'm so sorry but Dad—

I don't know how to tell you this, but your father—

Or, simply, *Dad died—*

She cannot think properly, she thinks.

The brain is a three-pound bag of neurons, electrical pulses, chemical messengers, and glial cells, Philip likes to lecture Louise during dinner. There's the right brain, the left brain, the four lobes: the frontal lobe, the occipital or the visual cortex, which is in the back of the brain—

Please, Dad, I'm eating.

You're not eating much, Philip says, looking over at her plate, before he continues. The parietal cortex, the temporal lobe, which is behind the ears—can you pass the broccoli, Nina? The lamb chops are delicious. The limbic system, the seat of emotion and memory, the brain stem, the seat of consciousness that keeps us awake or puts us to sleep at night. I wish they would teach the geography of the brain in schools the way they teach the geography of the world—Ecuador, Nigeria, Bulgaria, can you tell me where those countries are, Lulu? he asks.

Dad, please! Louise says.

We know that our brain functions have evolved to react to atoms in reliable ways but we still have no real understanding of the physical basis of consciousness in the brain, Philip goes on, glancing again at Louise's plate—aren't you going to eat your meat?—and this brings me back to the question—since we accept the Copenhagen interpretation of quantum mechanics—what does that cat inside the box experience consciously?

Oh, no, not that poor cat again, Nina says, interrupting.

Does the cat experience being alive and dead at the same time?—Are you listening, Lulu? Or is the cat dependent on someone opening the box and checking?

You mean for something to be real, it has to be observed? Louise asks, pushing away her plate.

Real in the perceivable universe, Philip says.

Okay, pass me your plate, Lulu, I'll eat the rest of your lamb chops, he also says.

Philip has a healthy appetite.

He will eat anything—rooster testicles, shark fin soup, garbanzo bean stew, crêpes coquilles St.-Jacques, the *daube de boeuf à la provençale* that she will cook for him one day.

She remembers the roast chicken congealing downstairs.

An appetite for—

life.

* * *

She takes his hand. His fingers are cold and stiff and she bends them around until they meet hers. Then she brings his hand up to her lips.

"If I say, 'I am 95 percent certain I locked the door before I left the house,'" Philip tells his students on the last day of class, "that is a classic example of epistemic probability—probability based on intuition. But if I say, 'I am 95 percent certain that I will die before my wife'—we all know that women tend to outlive men—this is called *a posteriori* probability—probability computed after an event. By taking a large sample, you can compute the probability—according to the law of large numbers—of all kinds of events: who will get sick when, who will die when, and so forth, within a desired degree of accuracy. However"—here Philip pauses significantly—"I strongly suggest that you stay vigilant. Probabilities can be very misleading. You must try to expect the unexpected. The event no one predicted—an epidemic, a tsunami—the event that will make an enormous difference.

"Let me give you the famous example of the turkey—the British use a chicken instead," Philip smiles. "Picture a turkey, a turkey who is fed regularly every morning for, say, a year. The turkey gets used to this routine. In fact, the turkey gets so used to it that he naturally comes to expect that every morning at a certain hour someone is going to come and feed him. But"—Philip starts to laugh—"one morning, maybe a week or so before Thanksgiving, that same person who comes and feeds the turkey every morning at pretty much the same time, instead of feeding him, wrings his neck.

"You see"—everyone in the class is laughing—"something unexpected happened that has completely altered our belief system and our reliance on past events. This raises the question of how can we predict the future by our knowledge of the past. These are important considerations that I want you to think about."

Philip's students stand up and clap.

In the Paris café, she does not look Philip in the face; she looks down at his neck. Sticking out of his open-collared blue shirt, she notices a little tuft of dark hair.

Her heart is pounding rapidly inside her chest.

Briefly, and however improbably, she wonders if she is having a heart attack.

Or else she is coming down with something—a grave illness.

Frowning, she looks away. She much prefers blond men to dark, hairy ones.

As if he can read her mind, he puts his hand up to his collar and buttons it. Then, holding out his hand, he says, I'm Philip.

The bedroom is getting lighter.

It is the hour before dawn that the ancient Romans called the hour of the wolf. The hour when demons have a heightened power and when most people die or children are born. The hour when people are gripped by nightmares.

L'heure bleue.

* * *

Hearing an unaccustomed sound in the bedroom—of something knocked down—Nina opens her eyes. The chair by the door with her beige cashmere sweater draped over it is lying on the floor. Someone has entered the room.

An angel.

The angel flaps his great wings.

The sound he makes is like *Hypatia*'s sails snapping and tearing in a high wind.

The angel is familiar.

He has the same curly red hair and black wings and he wears the same swirling piece of white cloth as the angel in Caravaggio's *Rest on the Flight into Egypt,* the painting that had transfixed her. At the time, she could not move away from it, nor could she explain why, and Philip became impatient. The painting, he said, was sentimental and he preferred the realism of the two Caravaggios they had seen in one of the chapels of Santa Maria del Popolo. And it was lunchtime. But on the way from the Palazzo Doria Pamphili to the restaurant, Philip's wallet was stolen. Only after they had eaten and it was time to pay did he notice that it was gone.

His great black wings outstretched, the angel comes and stands next to her by the bed. He puts out his hand to Nina.

Where is it? Nina asks. She is thinking of the wallet.

Smiling, the angel shakes his head.

She must be dreaming.

It does not matter.

She is neither frightened nor surprised.

Nina takes the angel's hand and she lets him lead her over to the window. The angel pulls back the curtains and opens the window wide. Fresh air streams into the bedroom. The sun is shining and it is a beautiful, clear day. Below, in the garden, a little wet still from the rain, the lilacs and peonies are in bloom. Nina takes a deep breath. From where she stands, she can smell the lilacs. French lilacs. Then, as her eyes grow accustomed to the light, she can make out Philip.

Dressed in his blue work shirt, the sleeves rolled up to his elbows, he is already out in the vegetable garden—hoeing, planting, weeding. When he sees Nina at the bedroom window, he stops what he is doing and, straightening up tall, he waves to her.

ACKNOWLEDGMENTS

Like the despised magpie who shamelessly steals from other birds' nests to line her own, I have done so on page 18, from E. T. Jaynes, *Probability Theory: The Logic of Science* (Cambridge University Press, 2003, p. 1); on page 26, from Mary-Louise von Franz, *Psyche and Matter* (Shambala, 1992); on page 40 and again on page 110, from Morris Kline, *Mathematics for the Nonmathematician* (Dover Publications, 1985, pp. 524–26); on page 46, from Simon Singh, *The Code Book* (Doubleday, 1999, pp. 260–61); on page 56, from Adam Phillips, *Monogamy* (Vintage,1996, p. 105); on page 79 and again on page 124, Lorna's conversation is paraphrased from Janna Levin, *How the Universe Got its Spots* (Princeton University Press, 2002, pp. 1, 4, 7); on page 88 and again on page 126, from Frank Wilczek who won the Nobel Prize for Physics in 2004 and is currently the Herman Feshbach professor of physics at MIT and who with his wife, Betsy Devine, wrote *Longing for the Harmonies: Themes and Variations from Modern*

Physics (W.W. Norton & Co., 1989); on page 96, from Douglas Hofstadter, *I Am a Strange Loop* (Basic Books, 2007, p. 252); on page 107, from Keith Devlin, *The Unfinished Game: Pascal, Fermat, and the Seventeenth-Century Letter That Made the World Modern* (Basic Books, 2009, pp. 2, 9, 25–26, 29); on page 125, from Stephen Hawking, *A Brief History of Time* (Bantam, 1988, pp. 148–50); on page 127, from Patricia Lynne Duffy, *Blue Cats and Chartreuse Kittens: How Synesthetes Color Their World* (Times Books/Henry Holt, 2001, p. 22); on page 138, lyrics quoted from the Great Courses recording *The Joy of Mathematics*, lecture 12, *The Joy of Pi*, taught by Arthur T. Benjamin (he attributes the lyrics to Larry Lesser, a friend); on page 139, from the Great Courses recording *What Are the Chances? Probability Made Clear*, taught by Michael Starbird; on page 150 and again on page 184, from an interview with William Kentridge by Michael Auping in *William Kentridge: Five Themes* (San Francisco Museum of Art and Norton Museum of Art in association with Yale University Press, pp. 230–245); on page 161, from John Berger, *From A to X* (Verso, 2008); and on page 178, from John Berger, *Ways of Seeing* (Penguin, 1972); on page 184, from Richard Feynman, *Six Easy Pieces* (Basic Books, 1963, p. 5); and on page 187, from Nassim Nicholas Taleb, *The Black Swan: The Impact of the Highly Improbable* (Random House, 2007, p. 40).

I also want to acknowledge the various Internet sites I have used for information: http://mathworld.wolfram.com/LawofLargeNumbers.html; http://gwydir.demon.co.uk/jo/probability/info.htm; http://members.chello.nl/r.kuijt/en_pi_onthouden.htm; www.cl.cam.ac.uk/research/hvg/Isabelle/overview.html; and www.templeton.org/pdfs/articles/Physics_World_Faraday07.pdf.

My special thanks to Nathaniel Kahn for his keen observations and explanations. *Un grand merci* to Irène Bungener and Bertrand Duplantier. For their friendship, advice, and support, I want to thank Molly Haskell, Michelle Huneven, Frances Kiernan, and Patricia Volk. I am also greatly indebted to Trent Duffy for his editing of this book. As always, I thank Georges and Anne Borchardt. And, finally, I want to thank my most gracious and excellent editor Elisabeth Schmitz.